Three Treasures

Three Treasures

Countdown Chronicles No. 2

Nikki Bennett

FIREDRAKE BOOKS, LLC
Set your imagination on fire

Three Treasures

Dedication

This book is dedicated to my mother. Thanks for
being my inspiration!

Contents

ONCE THERE LIVED a brother and sister who could not get along. They argued about everything: who was the smartest, who was the best looking, who was loved more.

One day, the brother proposed a contest to end the arguments once and for all. But when the sister won the contest, the brother got mad and another fight began.

So, the sister ran away. She hid in a cave and the world went dark. For the sister was Goddess of the Sun, and while she hid, no light would fall on the Earth.

Finally, the goddess ventured from her cave and her brother apologized by giving her a gift: his own sword.

Much later, the Sun Goddess gave the sword to her grandson. She also bequeathed to him a mirror and a jewel of great beauty. She sent her grandson down to Earth to aid the people there.

AND SO, THE Three Sacred Treasures left the heavens. The gods brought them to a long, snaky island full of mountains and volcanoes. An island where the ground rumbled and the seas boiled. The Treasures were never seen in heaven again. They were kept on Earth, guarded and protected.

Until they day they disappeared.

I

The Rat Boy

Raahi was absolutely sure he was a god. He knew this because he lived in Deshnoke, a city in northern India, and this city had a temple dedicated exclusively to rats. Thousands of black rats made the temple their home, along with a few special white ones rumored to be the reincarnated family of the great goddess Karni Mata. If you caught a glimpse of these pure white rodents, the goddess would bless you, and she especially honored you if a rat ran across your bare feet as you walked through the temple.

A few months ago, a new animal appeared in the temple. Brilliant white fur covered this rat, and green eyes sparkled in its tiny face. Murmurs circulated that the rodent was the reincarnation of Karni Mata herself. No one had ever seen a rat with green eyes. She was a special animal indeed.

People from all over traipsed to Deshnoke to catch a glimpse of the elusive rat, but it avoided all contact. It refused to run over worshipper's feet or lap milk from a bowl with its human subordinates like the other rats. It scuttled out every so often, enough for the excited worshippers to catch a swift peek. But no one could get near it.

Then Raahi entered the temple.

He came with his father, who hoped to catch a fleeting glimpse of Karni Mata. Raahi didn't care about the rat. He was thinking of more important things that day. Two kids at school had borrowed money from him and he was busy deciding the meanest way to get the money back. Beating them up after class, maybe. Or sending some well-phrased threats. He pondered his options as he followed his father into the temple.

They meandered over the cool tiles. Rats scurried across their path. They passed a large metal bowl filled with milk; rats and humans drank together, a solemn ritual. They passed men sitting in serene contentment against the wall. Rats scuttled over their shoulders, down their arms, and across their laps.

Raahi's father sat against the wall also.

"Maybe," he whispered, "if we are still and quiet, we will see the special rat."

Raahi sighed and sank down beside his father. He stared sullenly at the far wall where a few rats nibbled some fruit. Behind the fruit, two eyes peered from a hole in the wall.

Two sparkling green eyes.

Raahi's eyes grew wide. The pure white reincarnation of Karni Mata emerged and scuttled towards him. Gasps echoed through the room. Then, everyone fell silent.

She was a beautiful creature. White fur glowed in the dim light, dainty pink feet glided over the tiles, and a graceful tail wavered in the gentle breeze. Her eyes locked with the boy's. She ran right up to Raahi and, while others stared in amazement, the great goddess rat climbed his leg and sat in his lap.

Raahi gazed into the rat's eyes, mesmerized. She stared back.

"Incredible," his father said.

Karni Mata's ears perked and she squeaked at the noise. She turned and bolted for her hole.

"She has blessed you," Raahi's father whispered.

Raahi fumed. "You scared her away." He wouldn't speak to his father for the rest of the day.

The next time he visited the temple, Raahi went alone. Again the rat chose him above the many others roaming the halls. She climbed his arm and sat on his shoulder. When a man, yearning for a glimpse, moved too close, the rat bolted for her hole. Raahi was only a boy, but that didn't stop him from scolding the man, who hung his head in shame.

Whenever Raahi visited the temple, Karni Mata would meet him. She never approached anyone else. The locals learned to stay away from the two. They watched from a respectful distance. And the more they gazed with reverence at Raahi and his rat, the more important Raahi felt.

He decided since Karni Mata chose him, he must be a reincarnated god too.

But which one?

Raahi wasn't that religious. Earthly things interested him more, like figuring out ways to scam money from kids at school, bullying classmates into doing his homework, even stealing from his favorite candy shop when he could. His parents both had good jobs, and he made a tidy sum from his victims on the playground so he didn't *need* to steal. But he stole anyway, just to see if he could get away with it. Besides, everyone knew the white rat favored him. Even the adults couldn't deny his greatness.

The kids at school learned about the rat and became fearful. When Raahi's gang spread the rumor that he was a reincarnated god, their fear ran deeper. Now if Raahi wanted money or homework he didn't resort to bullying. He didn't need to. Whatever he wanted, kids handed over without question.

So whether he really believed he was a god or not, it suited his purpose and he had no qualms pretending. He decided he must be Ganesh, the god with the elephant head.

Now when he entered the temple and the rat ran up to him, he didn't see a goddess in those emerald eyes. He saw a servant. For she wasn't as important as Ganesh. Even in her own temple, Raahi looked down on Karni Mata.

"You're just my servant," he told her. "Ganesh *rides* on a rat, you know."

The rodent squeaked. She scurried down his arm, sat on the floor, and groomed her paws.

Raahi glanced around. The few people present in the temple weren't looking his way. His eyes fell on the rat. He got to his feet. A crazy thought had entered his brain and now he couldn't get rid of it.

To prove his Ganesh theory, shouldn't he *ride* the rat? If she held up under his weight, he'd know for sure.

He didn't stop to consider that he'd squish the poor animal if he stepped on her. He took a step forward. The rat paid no attention. He glanced around the room again. The coast was still clear. He raised his right foot and lowered it onto the rat's head.

A small squeak issued from under his shoe. Then the rat fell silent.

Then, something incredible happened. Soft, pearly smoke billowed from under his foot. It filled the spaces around him until Raahi could see nothing but white. He sucked in his breath. Smoke filled his lungs. He coughed and tried calling for help, but besides the coughing, no sound came from his mouth. He couldn't move his legs. His hands tingled. Panic enveloped him but he couldn't run, couldn't escape the smoke. He crumpled to the floor.

A squeak and a low hiss filled his ears. The last things he saw were Karni Mata's green eyes. They grew into eyes belonging to an animal much, much larger than a rat. The eyes blinked, and he remembered no more.

2

The Girl and the Dog

KATE LAY ON her bed and nibbled her pencil.

She hated math. She stared at the paper until the numbers blurred. She threw her pencil down, sat up, tossed her long, auburn hair over her shoulder with one hand, and grabbed a lipstick tube with the other. She opened the empty tube. She'd used the lipstick up months ago, but she stared at the tube anyway, hoping.

The tube sparkled.

"Hello Kate. The words floated out of the tube. Kate smiled.

"Hi Jinjing. I hoped it'd be you."

"Really?" The voice sounded surprised. "Why?"

Kate laughed. She and Jinjing hadn't gotten along the last time they met, but Kate had mellowed since. Jinjing still wasn't her favorite person, but they shared a common bond. They went on a wild adventure together once, along with two boys: Pietro from Italy and Saburo from Japan. The only reminders of that adventure were the magical objects they kept.

On that adventure, a golden dragon had enchanted Kate's lipstick tube, Jinjing's barrette, Pietro's water bottle, and Saburo's wooden spoon. Once, these magical objects could provide fire, weapons, water, and food. Now they transmitted voices. Like a phone, with the added benefit that they translated languages. Since Saburo spoke Japanese and Pietro Italian, this helped a lot. Jinjing lived in Hong Kong and spoke English fluently.

"I'm stuck," Kate said. "How good are you at math?"

"Not so great. You should talk to Saburo. He's much better at math than me. He helped me with my homework last week."

Some of the old feelings Kate had towards Jinjing came back. Annoyance. A little jealousy?

No, that was silly. Saburo was as much Jinjing's friend as Kate's. There was no reason why he couldn't help Jinjing with her homework. Still, the idea irritated Kate for some reason. She took a deep breath.

"Thanks. I'll do that."

A sneeze echoed from somewhere near the foot of the bed. "What was that?" Jinjing asked.

"Oh," Kate said, "it's just Pug." She glanced towards the foot of the bed where a lump lay. The lump rolled over and snorted.

"When did you get a dog?"

"I didn't. My aunt brought him over for us to watch while she's on vacation."

Kate gazed at the pug in disgust. She had been excited when her father told her they'd be dog sitting. She'd always wanted a dog. But Pug, he wasn't what she'd had in mind.

The dog yawned, rolled over, and let out a stinky toot.

"Ew." Kate pinched her nose shut. "He's absolutely disgusting. He's gassy and slobbers, and all he does is eat and sleep. And he stares at me when he thinks I'm not looking."

Jinjing laughed. "*Stares* at you?"

"Yeah, I swear he does. When I'm getting ready for bed or when I'm lying here. Yesterday when I got out of the shower, there he was, standing in the bathroom doorway and *leering* at me."

Jinjing choked on her laughter. "You think you have a perverted dog on your hands?"

"Stop laughing, it isn't funny. He's the creepiest dog on the planet. And I'm stuck with him for another week." Kate threw a sock at the dog, but he just rolled over and snored.

"Worse, my aunt insists he sleep in my bed. He sleeps in her bed, and is just the *sweetest* companion. That's what *she* says, but I don't know how she can stand the thing. When I wake up, I'm covered in drool. The other night he pooped on my favorite shirt. He's horrible."

Jinjing laughed so hard at this, that Kate said goodbye in a bit of a huff, snapped the lipstick tube shut, and thrust it into her pocket. She frowned at the dog. His mouth hung open and a thin trickle of drool dripped onto her bedspread. She wrinkled her nose.

"Get up, you disgusting thing. Let's go get dinner."

Pug perked an ear at the mention of food. He rolled to the floor and wheezed as he plodded towards the door. Kate made a face and followed.

She roamed through the kitchen, searching for something tasty for dinner. Her mother, who had never liked cooking much, had left years ago and her father didn't know what a frying pan was. So, it fell on Kate to make dinner. She was becoming quite a good cook, but the pantry didn't hold much today. She settled for boiling some macaroni and cheese, and emptied a can of dog food in a bowl for Pug.

She brought some dinner to her father, who pounded at the keyboard in his study, like usual.

"Whatcha writing, Dad?"

He glanced at her. "A history book titled 'Lighthouses of the East Coast'."

"Sounds fascinating." Kate grinned, thinking *nothing* could be more boring than a book about lighthouses. She hoped her father wouldn't expect her to read it.

"Thanks hon," he said, not even glancing at the dinner. His fingers never stopped tapping on the keyboard.

"Dad, you gotta eat. You've been in here for hours."

Her father turned, his thin lips smiling up at her. "I'll eat it, precious. Thank you."

Kate rumpled his thinning hair and shuffled into the living room with her bowl. She plopped onto the couch, turned on the TV, and sighed.

A thump landed beside her. Pug had managed to clamber onto the sofa. He stared at her, dog food smeared across his face.

Kate made a gagging noise. "Ugh. You've even got some inside your ears, you ugly thing. How'd you manage to do that?"

Pug yawned and belched. "You are a disgrace to the entire dog species," Kate said.

Pug opened his mouth to yawn again. Kate flinched, waiting for the stink, but instead a pearly mist floated out Pug's mouth. She fumbled in her pocket and gripped the lipstick tube, a jolt of excitement coursing through her. Something was happening.

The dog stared at her. A sharp intensity filled those dopey round eyes. This was no ordinary dog. Kate gazed at Pug with a new respect. The mist surrounded her. She didn't try to avoid it. She knew what she had to do. She opened her mouth wide and breathed the mist in.

3

The Boy and the Fox

SABURO STARED AT his father's bones. They lay in a jumbled heap on the sterile steel cart. They had been burned white and clean. He gazed at them, not knowing what to think. He had never known his father. Taro, his eldest brother had, and Jiro had faint memories, but their father left right before Saburo's birth. He moved to Tokyo with his new wife and left his old family behind. When Saburo asked his mother why his father never wrote or visited, she just said *that's the way it is, Saburo* and wouldn't discuss it further.

Taro insisted they attend the funeral. So, they boarded the bullet train that would take them over six hundred kilometers to Tokyo.

Saburo had never been to Tokyo. He had wanted to do some sightseeing, but they wouldn't have time for it. Their mother had scrounged the money for the train tickets and they could only afford two nights in the hotel.

Now Saburo held a pair of long chopsticks in his hand. He glanced at a boy he didn't even know, a cousin of some sort, who held an identical pair of chopsticks. Together, they used the chopsticks to pick up a bone and place it in the urn. Then Saburo turned and handed the chopsticks to the next person in line. He joined his brothers who stood a little distance from Saburo's two half-brothers. Saburo looked at the boys. A stab of hatred shot through him.

These boys were both younger than himself, but they had the honor of placing their father's bones in the urn first. Before even Taro, the eldest, had the chance. Taro should have been first, but their father's new family took that important honor away. He hated them all. He hated his father too. He glared at the bones.

Anger bubbled inside him. Anger that he would never know his father now. Anger at his half-brothers who he probably would never talk to again once he climbed aboard the train and headed home. He gritted his teeth and wished the funeral would hurry up and end.

This was the last part: transferring the burnt bones to the urn. Yesterday had been the wake, this morning they covered his father's shrunken body with flowers and followed the hearse to the crematorium. They ate lunch while they waited. Then they were ushered into this small antechamber. The priest wheeled the burned bones in on the cart and the entire party took turns moving the bones into the urn, using the ceremonial chopsticks.

Saburo glanced at his brothers, wondering what they were thinking. Taro looked sad. Jiro, uncomfortable. Like Saburo, maybe he hoped it would all be over soon.

Saburo wanted to feel sorrow. Or at least some pity for his two half-brothers who cried in their mother's arms. But he couldn't. His father had abandoned him and never gave him a second thought. Why should he care about any of them?

He needed some time by himself. As the funeral party left the crematorium, Saburo broke away.

"Saburo!" Taro called. "Do you remember how to get to the hotel?"

"Yes!" Saburo said before he left them behind. He wandered down the street and walked until his hip throbbed in protest. He rubbed it. The remains of an old accident when he was younger, the annoying hip always acted up if he used it too much. He sat on a stoop and sighed.

His anger had ebbed during the walk. He glanced up the alley at the houses and shops all crammed together. He didn't see anyone. Most people were still at work or school. He pulled off his jacket and undid his tie. He hated dressing up; the itchy suit stuck to his skin. He thought about heading to the hotel so he could change.

He had no clue how to *get* to the hotel. He stared down the alley, feeling stupid for not paying any attention to where his feet took him. He pulled out three hundred yen in change from his pocket. That wouldn't be enough money for a taxi. He'd have to walk.

He stood, groaning, wishing he at least had been smart enough to carry a cell phone. He reached in his pocket again, and his hand closed around a key chain. He pulled it out.

Saburo's key chain had a key to his house and a wooden spoon dangling from a red thread. He got the spoon on Miyajima Island when he was younger, and later, when he went on that crazy adventure with Kate, Jinjing, and Pietro, a Yellow Dragon had enchanted it. He gripped the spoon now, knowing that if the others were holding their magical objects he could talk to them.

The spoon glowed. Pietro's voice spilled out of it.

"Hello?"

"Hello Pietro," Saburo said.

"Saburo, how are you?"

"Well, right now I'm lost in Tokyo. How about you?"

Pietro's yawn echoed off the spoon. "It's seven in the morning here. I was just about to leave for school. What are you doing in Tokyo?"

Saburo didn't feel like talking about the funeral, even to Pietro. He changed the subject. "Have you heard from the others lately?"

"Well, I talked to Jinjing last night. She had just talked to Kate."

Saburo's heart skipped at the mention of Kate. He wished he could talk to her more often, but they never seemed to hold their magical objects at the same time, which was the only way the objects would work. He sighed and stared down the alley.

Two green eyes blinked at him.

He thought the eyes must belong to a cat, but then he sucked in his breath. "Pietro, are you still there?"

"Yes," Pietro said. "What's going on?"

"There's a kitsune sitting in the road and staring right at me."

"A what?"

"A kitsune. A fox. Right in the middle of Tokyo." Saburo squinted. The fox swished her tail.

No, *tails*.

"Pietro," Saburo said, "something's happening here."

"Something what?" Pietro said, sounding excited.

"The kitsune. She has six tails."

"*Six*?"

Saburo nodded, forgetting Pietro couldn't see him. He stared at the fox. Six thick, wavy tails fanned behind her. She gave Saburo a pointed stare, turned, and moved down the alley.

"I think she wants me to follow her."

"Then you'd better," Pietro said.

Saburo limped after the waving tails. A kitsune. A real, enchanted kitsune, here in Tokyo. He tried to remember everything he could about the magical animal. Kitsunes could be good and loyal, or mischievous and tricky. The more tails a kitsune had, the more knowledge it possessed. The most possible was nine so the six-tailed kitsune Saburo now followed must be clever indeed.

The alley ended at a wall. The kitsune stopped and turned to face him. Saburo gazed into her beautiful green eyes, trying to understand what she wanted.

The fox opened her mouth. Smoke poured out. Saburo grabbed his spoon.

"Pietro, are you still there?"

"Yes," Pietro said. "What's happening?"

"Something crazy," Saburo sucked in a lungful of the white stuff and coughed. His hand clamped on his spoon. Pietro spoke, but the smoke clogged Saburo's ears and Pietro's voice faded.

Saburo shut his eyes. He relaxed. He waited for something incredible to happen.

4

Amaterasu

"Saburo, are you still there?"

Pietro's voice floated through a fog. Saburo blinked. The blurry greens and browns in the distance grew into trees, and a dark lump in the foreground hardened into a rock. He sat up.

"I'm not in Tokyo anymore," he whispered into the spoon. "I'm in the woods. I don't know where, though."

He gazed about. Tall pines surrounded a grassy glade filled with small purple flowers. Birds twittered and crickets chirped, but he didn't see another living thing.

"I'm all by myself, I think. I don't know where I am, or *when*, for that matter."

"But I can still hear you," Pietro said, "so wherever you are, or *whenever*, these magical objects still

17

work. Anyway, I have to go. I'm sorry, my father is yelling at me to get to breakfast. Keep your spoon close. I'll talk to you later."

"OK," Saburo said. "Let the others know if you can."

He put the spoon in his pocket, limped to the rock, and sat, lost in thought.

She walked into the glade.

Beautiful red hair floated around a pale face studded with blue eyes. He thought she might be a goddess, but goddesses wouldn't dress in jeans and sweatshirts.

"Kate-*chan*!"

"Saburo!" Kate ran forward and flung her arms around him. He braced against the rock, hoping he wouldn't fall over. Kate babbled on. "Oh I am so glad to see you. I thought I was all alone."

She let go and Saburo, a bit dazed, collected his thoughts. He hadn't understood all she had said. He had studied English hard since their last adventure, but still had trouble with the language. But Kate smiled. She was glad to see him. He understood *that*.

"How…how are you?" he said in passable English.

Kate laughed. "You're learning! I'm OK. A little confused right now, but OK."

Saburo frowned, not catching all her words. Then he grinned, pulled out his spoon, and put it up to his ear. A flash of understanding shot through Kate's eyes. She pulled out her lipstick tube.

"Now say something," Saburo said in Japanese.

"I understand you," Kate laughed. "Can you understand me?"

"Perfectly," Saburo said.

"Where do you think we are?"

Saburo shrugged. "I don't know. I wonder where the kitsune went."

"Kitsune?"

"The fox. She breathed a white smoke on me, and I woke up here."

Kate sucked in her breath. "The same thing happened to me. Except an ugly pug dog breathed on me. Who really, I'm thinking, wasn't a pug dog after all. Do you think the others will come? Pietro and Jinjing, I mean?"

"I just talked to Pietro," Saburo said. "He was heading off to school."

Kate frowned. "And I talked to Jinjing right before Pug breathed on me, but I don't see her anywhere. I wonder why *we're* here."

A cough echoed from between the trees. Saburo spun around. "Who's there?"

A small boy stepped into the glade. Younger than Saburo and Kate, the boy walked through the grass barefoot.

"Who are you?" Kate asked. "And where are your shoes?"

The boy didn't answer. Saburo pulled off his hot jacket and choking tie, threw them on the rock, and studied the new boy. He had black hair and sallow skin. Two brown eyes stared at Saburo with a mixture of interest and aloofness. A large nose jutted from his face. He had a small, wiry body. He was even shorter than Saburo, who wasn't that tall.

"Hello," Kate said, waving her hand around. "Do you speak English?

"Yes," the boy said.

"Good," Kate said. "Because we don't have a magical translator for you."

"A what?"

"Never mind. My name is Kate, and this is Saburo. What's your name?"

The boy frowned. "My name…is Ganesh."

"Are you named Ganesh after the god?"

Saburo prodded Kate's shoulder. "What's Ganesh?"

"He's a Hindu elephant god," Kate said. "You've never heard of him?"

"No," Saburo said, feeling stupid.

Kate grinned. "Don't worry. The only reason I know is 'cause we have an Indian restaurant up the road called Ganesh. They serve the best curry on the planet."

"I am not named after the god," the boy said. "I *am* Ganesh."

Kate stared at the new kid. "If you're Ganesh, where's your tusks and trunk? And why aren't you wearing shoes?"

The boy glanced at his feet. "I took them off before I entered the temple."

"Well, you don't look like a god to me," Kate said. "You look like a boy. And I don't think your name is Ganesh. What is it?"

The boy shot her a sullen look, folded his arms, and refused to answer.

"Fine. I'll just call you 'Boy' then." She turned to Saburo. "I hope we're not stuck with this dweeb," she whispered.

Saburo grinned and studied the boy, who didn't seem too friendly. Saburo would have much rather been on this adventure with just Kate, if they couldn't have Pietro and Jinjing also. He wasn't happy to admit someone new into their circle, especially a bratty little boy.

"What do we do now?" he said. "I don't see a path through these woods so we can't go anywhere."

"Maybe we're supposed to meet somebody here," Kate said.

"But where are they?"

Kate shrugged. "Maybe they're running late."

"Somebody's coming," the Indian boy said.

Saburo's eyes followed the boy's pointing finger. A golden light fell between the trees and moved towards them. Kate slipped her hand into Saburo's and squeezed. His nervousness disappeared as he squeezed back.

The light crept into the glade and transformed the green grass into wavering slivers of gold so bright that Saburo had to shut his eyes. When he opened them, he saw her.

She stood at the glade's edge. Silver hair fell about her soft white face. Amber eyes studied them. The air was perfectly still around Saburo, but a breeze billowed the woman's long, white dress about her and ruffled her hair.

"I am Amaterasu," she said. Her voice sounded like beautiful music, but it didn't stop a chill from running right up Saburo's spine. He sucked in his breath.

"What?" Kate said. "You know who she is?"

"She's the sun goddess," Saburo said.

The Indian boy sidled next to Kate. "What did she say? I can't understand."

"That's 'cause you don't have a magical object." Kate held up her lipstick tube. "*I* can understand her."

"So can I," Saburo said, staring at the beautiful goddess.

Amaterasu trained her eyes onto Saburo. "You know me. You are from my country."

"Yes," Saburo said.

"Then you will understand my task. The Three are missing."

Saburo's mind whirred as he tried to grasp her meaning. "I'm sorry. What are the Three?"

"The Three Treasures protecting this land."

"Oh…that Three." Saburo's face grew hot with embarrassment. The Three Treasures of Japan belonged to the Emperor. The mirror, *Yata no Kagami*, and the jewel, *Yasakani no Magatama*, were only brought out for great ceremonies. Normal citizens never got to gaze upon these treasures. But the sword, *Kusanagi*, was lost during the great Battle of Dan-no-ura, centuries ago although several rumors swirled around this artifact. No one knew for sure who had it.

"So they *do* exist," Saburo said.

"They do. But they have been stolen."

"Let me guess. We're supposed to find them for you," Kate said.

The goddess fixed her eyes on Kate. Kate held her gaze. Saburo wasn't sure whether to scold Kate for waging a staring contest with a goddess or to commend her for it.

"I don't get it," Kate said. "You're a goddess. Why can't you get these things back yourself?"

"They have been taken away from this land," Amaterasu said, "and I cannot leave it."

"The Yellow Dragon couldn't leave his island either," Kate said. "Why?"

"Kate, this might not be the right time to ask these questions," Saburo said.

"But I want to know. It seems the monsters or fiends or whatever they are who *steal* these things can travel to any place they want, but the great gods and god-desses they steal from *can't*. Why?"

"I am bound to this land," Amaterasu said, "and I cannot leave it. But I will send some companions with you who can help you find the Treasures."

She waved her hand towards the woods. Three odd animals shuffled out.

"There's my kitsune," Saburo said. He recognized the green eyes and the six waving tails.

A huge cat strolled next to the kitsune. Black and white swirls covered its body, ending in a swirly tail that forked into one pure white tail and one tail black as night. The humongous cat's bright green eyes stared at them as its tails swished through the air.

Saburo gulped. "That's a bakeneko."

"A what?" Kate said.

"A bakeneko. A Monster Cat."

"I know those eyes," the new boy said. "They belong to Karni Mata. My rat."

"And I know *those* eyes." Kate glared at the third animal who was busy scratching himself. "Those are Pug's eyes or my name isn't Kate."

Saburo laughed. "That's a tanuki. A raccoon dog."

Kate wrinkled her nose as the tanuki let out a big belch and yawned. "Why are you laughing? There's nothing funny about that thing."

"Well, the Tanuki spirit likes to have a good time. He is a happy spirit. In my country most restaurants and bars have the tanuki's statue outside, to welcome their customers in. I always thought tanukis were funny."

"This one isn't. He's disgusting," Kate said. "If he's anything like Pug, all he'll want to do is eat, sleep, and poop."

"These spirits will help you in your quest," the goddess said. They will protect and guide you. The kitsune will accompany the boy from my country."

"That's me," Saburo said.

"The bakeneko will aid you." Amaterasu leveled her gaze at the Indian boy. He frowned.

"What did she say?"

"You get the cat, Boy," Kate said. "Which means I'm stuck with the stinky raccoon."

"Raccoon-dog," Saburo said. "He's not an American-type raccoon."

"The tanuki is wise and fearless and will serve you well," Amaterasu said.

The fat raccoon-dog let out a squeaky yawn and flopped on the ground. Kate wrinkled her nose. "Whatever you say."

Saburo decided they'd better get down to business. He wanted to know the particulars of this adventure. "Do you know who stole the Treasures?"

Amaterasu stared at Saburo. He wanted to squirm under her gaze, but forced himself to stand still.

"Yeah, you have to give us *something* to work with," Kate said. "How will we know where to go?"

"I do not know who stole the Treasures," the goddess said. "But they left their marks behind. You will find them. Your guides will help you when you are ready."

"Anything else?" Kate said.

Amaterasu tilted her head. "Else?"

"I mean, on our last adventure the Yellow Dragon gave us magical things to help us out. He gave us the worms that protected us. He enchanted objects so we could get food, water, fire, and weapons."

"Your guides will help you obtain all you require," the goddess said.

Kate gazed at her tanuki, dead asleep in the grass. "Are you sure about that?"

"I must leave," the goddess said. "When you find the Treasures, bring them to this glade. They will be safe here."

She floated away between the trees, and the golden light drifted off with her.

"Great," Kate said. "She hasn't given us poop to go on. We have to find these Treasures, either steal them back or fight whoever stole 'em, and bring 'em here. And all I've got for help is a stupid, useless raccoon-dog."

"Tanukis are clever," Saburo said. "He might surprise you."

"I hope he surprises me fast. And what are we supposed to do about this new kid? The one who thinks he's a god?"

"I can understand *you*," the new kid said.

"Sorry. Are you gonna to tell me your real name or not?"

"If you tell me what is going on," the boy said.

They filled him in on the scant details. He told them his name, Raahi, but insisted he was really the reincarnation of Ganesh. Saburo decided he didn't like the boy. He had shifty eyes. He acted much too calm considering he had never been on an adventure like this before. And he kept staring at Kate. Saburo didn't like *that* one bit.

He turned to his kitsune. "What do we do now?"

The fox blinked and vanished. In her place stood a beautiful chestnut horse with six long, red tails and two bright eyes. Saburo grinned.

"Holy cow," Kate said. "What just happened?"

"She's a shape-shifter," Saburo said. "We have to ride."

He glanced at the other animals. Raahi's bakeneko had morphed into a tall white steed with swirly black spots. And the tanuki…

"Oh great." Kate grimaced at the fat brown pony yawning and stretching in the grass. "How am I supposed to keep up with you two on that thing?"

"I've never ridden before," Raahi said, sounding nervous.

"I don't think it will matter," Saburo said in his halting English. "I think they will not let us fall. They will take us to where the Treasures disappeared. Let's go."

5

Tengu

THE BIRD CIRCLED high in the sky and scanned the ground, its sharp eyes searching. White feathers ruffled behind it as it dove towards the ground. It lit on a rock, opened its long, red beak, screeched, and ruffled its feathers.

No, not feathers—robes. For the bird disappeared and a grotesque man stood on the rock instead. The man sniffed the air with a nose that looked a lot like the bird's beak, except rounder on the end. He tucked in his flapping robes and stepped off the rock, still sniffing.

This man might not have been so ugly if his face and nose weren't such a bright red. He had white hair, like the bird's feathers. Bushy white eyebrows lined angry eyes. A perpetual frown hung underneath the long, bulbous nose. He dropped to all fours and shuffled across the stony ground crab-style, snuffling the rocks like a dog on the scent.

He sniffed every stone, tree, flower, and shrub. He didn't stop until his nose guided him to a steaming pit.

White sulfur oozed from the pit. Every time a bubble broke the gooey surface, a nasty smell of rotten eggs burst into the air. The heat from the sulfur caused the creature's large nose to wrinkle in disgust, but at the same time a twisted grin forced his frown slightly upwards. He stopped at the pit and crouched.

And there he waited.

<<<>>>

SABURO WISHED FOR two things.

One: he wished he had worn comfy clothes. Riding on Kitsune's back was not unpleasant. Although she bounded back and forth in a rocking motion, he found he was in no danger of sliding off. But his pants itched and his dress shoes pinched. He thanked the gods that he had left his tie and coat behind in the glade, but he wished for jeans, sneakers, and maybe a soft cotton t-shirt instead of the starchy dress shirt he wore.

Two: he wished Pietro and Jinjing were here. He missed them both, Pietro especially. After their experiences with legendary monsters, gods, and fiends, Pietro had come up with a theory.

Mythological creatures were real, Pietro said, but they lived on another plane of existence. So if Pietro were right, Saburo now rode across Japan, but not the Japan humans could see. In this Japan lived every spirit, ghoul, fairy, and monster in every myth he'd heard since infancy. They were real here and humans weren't. Except for Saburo, Kate, Jinjing, Pietro, and now Raahi, no human had ever set foot in this dimension. That's what Pietro would say.

The thought made Saburo shudder. He remembered plenty of scary monsters from childhood nightmares that he didn't much care to meet. And they were all skulking around in this other-Japan. He thanked Amaterasu for sending good spirits to guide them.

Although, now he thought about it, the bakeneko *did* have a tendency to eat humans on occasion, and the kitsune could be devious and sly. And Tanuki enjoyed playing pranks on people just to make them look stupid. Saburo wished Amaterasu had sent them an Oni as a guide. Oni may be demons, but they were big and strong and helpful when they felt like it.

Pietro also believed this mythological dimension's inhabitants could cross boundaries and enter the human world. This was how myths and legends came about in the first place. People caught glimpses and made up stories about the spirits, most stories hitting pretty far off the mark. But the crossing of boundaries happened rarely, which was why most people believed these creatures didn't exist.

Saburo thought Pietro's idea made sense. Pietro had many other theories, another reason why Saburo wished he were here. Instead, they were stuck with the new boy who knew nothing about anything. Saburo turned and studied the kid.

RAAHI'S MIND FOCUSED on something else entirely. He was more and more convinced that all this was happening because of his reincarnation status. It made perfect sense. He had tried to ride the rat, and the rat brought him to the land of gods. He *belonged* in this world. He ranked higher than all the mere humans in his old world.

He even had a good explanation for why the other kids were here too. Karmi Mata must have brought Saburo and Kate here to act as his servants. Every god needed a few of those. Raahi wasn't sure how he could use Saburo, except maybe to wait on him when he needed it. But he could fantasize a couple of good uses for Kate. He pictured her feeding him grapes and fanning him with a big leaf, like the slave girls used to do in the olden days. He glanced over his shoulder and watched Kate's fiery hair float in the wind.

KATE WASN'T THINKING of anything except how slow and stumbly her pony was. She hoped they reached their destination before Tanuki decided he had enough running and wanted to take another nap.

"WHAT'S THAT UP ahead?" Kate asked.

"Maybe it's a fire," Raahi said.

Saburo watched the steam rise into the air. "No, that's not fire-smoke. It could be a volcano."

"It's not coming from a mountain though," Kate said. "It's right below us."

Their "horses" turned down a path and descended towards the rising steam. Kate gazed at the blue sea in the distance, island after island breaking its surface.

"Beautiful," she said. "Saburo, Japan is so beautiful. You live in the prettiest country ever."

Saburo grinned. He thought of his village: the tiled houses, boxy buildings, and his mountain rising behind it. He liked living in the country. In big cities like Tokyo, you could go for days without seeing a mountain, except for Mt. Fuji when it wanted to show itself. On most days Fuji-san hid behind a wall of fog and nobody saw it. Saburo had been disappointed when he and his brothers had reached Tokyo without even catching a glimpse of the fabled mountain.

Here, the mountains were smaller but more plentiful. They fell towards the sparkling sea.

"I think that steam is coming from a sulfur pit," he said.

"A what?"

"A sulfur pit. Japan's full of them. This place looks a lot like Beppu, except there's no houses."

"Beppu?"

Saburo nodded. "A town on the island of Kyushu. Remember, about an hour ago when our…um…*horses* swam across that small strait?"

Kate nodded. Tanuki had plopped into the water so hard, she'd been doused from head to foot. Her clothes were finally starting to dry.

"That was the Kammon Strait. It's the spot where the Battle of Dan-no-ura was fought, way back. It separates Japan's mainland from this island. Beppu is a resort town. It has tons of hot springs and spas. I bet that's where we are now."

"Mmm, spa," Kate said. "Sounds good. But I don't see any houses. Haven't you noticed, we've seen no people at all. You think we're back in a time before people existed?"

"No."

Saburo turned his head around. The "no" had come from the sullen boy riding the black and white horse. Saburo had been talking mostly Japanese so he was surprised Raahi had followed the conversation, especially since the new boy didn't have a translator like he and Kate had. But Rashi had managed to put together the pieces.

"We aren't back in time," Raahi said. "We're in the Land of the Gods."

"It looks like Japan to me," Saburo said in English. "But I think you're right."

Kate's eyes widened. "You do?"

Saburo nodded. "It's like Pietro said, Kate. This looks like Japan, but it isn't. That's why there are no people."

"Except us," Kate said.

"I'm not people. I'm a god," Raahi said.

"Yeah, yeah, we know." Kate rolled her eyes and grinned at Saburo. "But *we're* not. And if this is the land of the gods, why are *we* here?"

Saburo leaned back as Kitsune picked her way down a steep trail. "Maybe we're here because the gods let us in. We're special."

Kate turned her head towards Raahi. "Got that, boy?"

"No," Raahi said, sounding rankled at Kate's use of the word "boy."

Kate turned to Saburo. "*We're* special," she whispered, "but why's *he* here?"

Their horses made it down the mountain and approached the steamy pit. Kate pointed at the shaowy figure stooped over the pit.

"What's that?"

"You mean 'who's' that," Raahi said. "That's a man."

"He's sure an ugly man."

Saburo studied the red face and the billowing white robes. "I think that's a Tengu."

"And a Tengu is—?"

"A guardian spirit. He protects the woods and mountains. We *must* be in the land of the gods."

Saburo nodded. "Raahi is right. This *is* the land of the gods. They've brought us here for some reason. I bet we're the only humans ever to see this place, even though it looks like our world except without people."

"Don't say 'Raahi is right' too much," Kate said, glancing over her shoulder at the boy who strained his his ears to hear their conversation. "He might start to believe it."

They dismounted. The horses morphed into Kitsune, who curled up daintily in a patch of grass; Bakeneko, who began cleaning her paws; and Tanuki, who flopped on the ground and rolled in the dirt, his tongue lolling out his mouth.

Saburo approached the spirit on the rock and bowed. "Tengu-san?"

The figure nodded. Saburo studied his glaring eyes and frowning mouth. He sure wasn't a *happy* spirit.

Tengu didn't speak. He pointed at Saburo with a claw-like finger and pulled an object from his robes. Saburo stared as Tengu placed it in his hands. He held it up.

"What's that?" Kate said.

"I don't know." Saburo said, rolling it about on his palm. Small and golden, it glinted in the watery sunlight.

"I know what that is," Raahi said. "It's a dorje."

"A what?"

"A dorje. It's what the Buddha holds in his hand. You see it all the time in Buddhist temples."

"Are you a Buddhist?"

"No," Raahi said, "I'm Hindu. But I have seen statues of Buddha. He always holds the dorje."

Saburo wanted to smack himself in the forehead. Raahi was right. Now the Indian boy had pointed it out, he remembered seeing this object in temples. Saburo's family *was* Buddhist, he should have known immediately about the dorje. Why did Tengu give it to him? What was he supposed to do with it?

"It is time," Tengu said. His piercing voice sounded like an eagle's angry scream.

"Time for what?"

"Time to begin the journey. Keep it safe." Tengu nodded at the dorje clutched in Saburo's hand. "You will need it to accomplish your task."

Saburo almost asked what his task was, but figured he knew. Like the last adventure, he had to find which spirit stole the Treasure, fight it, and get the Treasure back. He had no idea which Treasure he needed to find or how to fight the fiend who stole it, but he was ready. He had done this before.

"How do we get to where we're going?"

Tengu pointed his long nose at the steamy pit of boiling sulfur. "That is the way out."

Kate stared at the sulfur. "Ew. We don't have worms to protect us this time. How're we supposed to jump in a stinky, bubbling pit and not get burned to a crisp?"

"Your protectors will help," Tengu said.

Saburo gazed at Kitsune. She looked completely unconcerned at the idea of jumping into a crevice filled with oozy, stinking crud. She yawned and trotted over.

Kate reached for Saburo's hand. Warmth spread up his arm as she squeezed his fingers.

"I don't want to go in there," she whispered. "Remember the volcano on our last adventure? Remember Pele?"

"I remember. But you got through that OK. You'll be fine."

Kate shuddered. "I wish I had Bo with me."

Saburo nodded. He wished his protective worm, Oni, was here too. On their last adventure, their worms cocooned the kids in their bodies. They could swim at the bottom of the sea or crawl through lava-filled volcanos and not drown or burn. But how could the three animals standing before them protect them from boiling sulfur?

Tanuki scratched his rear end and waddled over to Kate, who took a step away and wrinkled her nose. The raccoon-dog ignored her attempts to escape. He prodded the back of her knees with his wet nose.

"Ew, stop it," Kate said. "What's he doing?"

Saburo laughed. "I think he wants you to jump in the pit."

"Heck, no. I'm not going into that stinky thing."

"You will be safe," Tengu said.

Raahi stepped closer to the pit. "What did he say?"

"He said to jump in," Saburo said. "He said we'll be safe."

Kate kicked back at Tanuki and refused to budge. "How 'bout you try it then, new kid?"

Raahi stood close to the pit. Small beads of sweat rolled down his face, but he took a step forward anyway.

"I'm not serious," Kate said. "Get away from there."

"No," Raahi said. "The spirit wants us to jump into this pit. The spirit says we will not be harmed. And I am a god. I cannot be harmed."

"Like fun you can't," Kate said. "You're just a pip-squeak kid. You're as much a god as I am."

Raahi glanced at Bakeneko. The large cat had padded to the sulfur pit and poked at the gooey white stuff with one paw. "It isn't hurting the cat," he said.

"Doesn't mean it won't hurt *you*," Kate said.

Raahi shrugged. "If the sulfur doesn't hurt the cat, and the cat is a spirit, it won't dare hurt me. I'm a god." He climbed to the edge of the boiling pit and stuck a foot in. "See? It isn't hot."

"Serious?" Kate inched closer.

"Jump in," Tengu said.

Raahi turned his head around. "What did he say?"

"Jump in," Saburo said in English. "If you dare."

Raahi's face broke into a grin. He turned to face the pit, took one deep breath, and jumped. He sunk beneath the ooze. The bakeneko hopped in after him.

Saburo turned to Kate. "Well," he said, "looks like it worked."

Kate frowned. "How do we know? How do we know Raahi didn't suffocate on his way down?"

Saburo didn't think this would happened. He knew Kate didn't believe it either. They had been through stranger situations than this. He glanced at Tengu. The ugly man bowed and whipped his long cloak around him. The wispy cloak disappeared and a huge bird with a long, red beak fluttered its wings and soared into the sky.

"Holy cow, he's a bird," Kate said, watching the Tengu-bird circle overhead.

Saburo gestured to the pit. "You go next, Kate."

Kate took a step backwards. "Why me? Why don't you go?"

"Because you're more scared of it than me. If I leave you here, what if you decide not to follow?"

Kate took a deep breath. "Well, I won't want to stay here alone, that's for sure. OK, already," she said, trying to kick Tanuki again as the animal rammed her legs. "I'm going."

She climbed over the rocks and dipped a finger into the ooze. "Cripes, it stinks. But it isn't hot. Not when you get right up to it." She took another deep breath, let out a little yelp, and jumped. Tanuki fell in behind her.

Saburo stared at the place where Kate had disappeared. A big bubble oozed out of the sulfur and popped, and a disgusting stench filled the air.

"Gross. Was that the sulfur or Tanuki? Ready, Kitsune?"

The fox swished her tails and pattered over the rocks. Saburo followed. He took a deep breath. He jumped.

6

Jigme

THE BOY LIVED in a beautiful valley. All around him, huge Himalayan peaks jutted into the sky, snow covering their tops. But in his valley, spring had begun.

Winter wheat wavered in the rice paddies. A meandering river cut through the valley, its banks lined with willow trees. Red and white flowers covered the rhododendron bushes growing along the dirt road.

The boy walked down the road and whistled. A dog's bark answered and a yellow mutt with muddy fur darted up the road to meet him.

"Hello, my friend," the boy said, scratching the dog behind its ears. He resumed his walk, the dog trotting beside him, and let his eyes drift to the temple on the hill. A long line of boy monks-in-training headed towards the temple for evening prayers. Their orange robes fluttered behind them as they walked. He didn't envy them. Boys who wanted to become monks had to learn so many lessons and they rarely had time to run free through the fields like he did.

Today he had no school and had played all afternoon. He wasn't concerned that he had no other kids to play with. The dog made a perfect playmate. When they weren't exploring the fields for insects or small animals, the boy took a book down to the river to read, and the dog lay next to his feet and panted. Today, the boy had a backpack slung across his shoulder, stuffed with a good book and a bottle of water. He crunched on smoky, roasted rice grains called *zaw* as he walked home.

He left the main road and trudged along a thin trail rising between the rice paddies. The trail was a shortcut to the main road. But before he got halfway down the trail, he stopped dead in his tracks. The dog barked and bolted. The boy blinked at the three shadowy shapes heading his way.

Yaks. He recognized them by their curved horns and long, fluffy tails, but these yaks weren't like any he'd ever seen. One had red hair and six (*six!*) of the bushiest yak tails he'd ever seen. Black and white swirls covered another beast. The third yak had brown fur and black rings around its eyes. But he noticed something even odder about these animals.

Kids rode on their backs.

Boys rode two of them, but the middle yak (which weaved from side to side and kept its mouth open in a constant yawn) carried a beautiful girl with porcelain skin and flowing red hair.

"Hello!" the girl called. "Speak English?"

The boy gulped and nodded. He backed away from the lumbering animals. He'd had a bad experience with an angry yak when he was six and didn't want to relive the experience.

The animals stopped a few feet away. The kids on their backs slid to the ground. The girl strode up to him. He shrunk back a couple more steps.

"Hi, I'm Kate." She stuck out a hand. "What's your name?"

The boy licked his lips and reached out a shaking hand to grasp hers. "Jigme."

Kate grinned. "Nice to meet ya. This is Saburo, by the way."

"Oh. Hello."

Saburo nodded. One hand gripped a small golden object. He reached out his other hand to shake Jigme's. "Hello," he said.

"And this is Raahi." Kate jerked her head towards the boy who gazed around at the scenery, ignoring the others.

"Raahi. That's an Indian name," Jigme said.

"Yup. And where are we?"

"What?"

Kate grinned. "What *country* are we in? Sorry, but we just got here you see."

Jigme frowned. The border between his country and India lay a few hundred kilometers down the valley. How could these kids have come all this way and not know where they were? And why were they riding yaks?

"You are in Bhutan," Jigme said. "This is the Land of the Thunder Dragon."

"Never heard of it," Kate said. "Are we in some place other than Earth? There isn't a land of a thunder dragon that I know of."

Raahi finally turned his head their way. "Yes there is. Bhutan is just above India. I've been here before."

"You have?"

"Yes, well, not right *here*. But I've been to Bhutan on holiday with my father. I've been to the capital, Thimphu."

"Thimphu is a long way from here," Jigme said. "It is over the mountains. Your yak is getting into the wheat."

"What?" Kate spun around. Tanuki had wandered off the path and now plowed through the paddy's soft dirt, trampling the winter wheat and yanking out huge mouthfuls.

"You'd better get him out of there," Jigme said. "My father will not be happy."

"Maybe your father can shoot him and serve him up as yak steak," Kate grumbled. She waded in and smacked Tanuki across his shoulder. "That'll fix my problems."

"No, we have no guns here. Bhutan is a peaceful Buddhist country. We do not kill our animals. They are free to wander where they please, but we do not want them messing up our crops."

"Too bad," Kate said, chasing the yak back to the path. "I've got a hankering for a good grilled yak steak."

Jigme turned to Raahi. "Where do you live in India?"

"Deshnoke. The girl is from America, and the boy is from Japan."

"What are you *doing* here?"

Raahi gave the boy an imperious glare. "We're here on the business of the gods."

"The what?"

Kate punched Raahi in the shoulder. "Shut up, boy, you're going to freak out the poor kid."

Raahi scowled. "You don't think he isn't already wondering why three foreigners are riding around his paddies on yaks?"

Jigme nodded. "It *is* strange although I've seen people ride them sometimes. But why are you here?"

Kate frowned. "Well, I wouldn't put it like Raahi, but we *are* here on 'spirit' business, I guess."

Jigme stared at the girl, wondering what on Earth she was talking about. Kate sighed.

"We're here to fight a demon and rescue a treasure so we can bring it back to the Japan spirit world." She turned red as she said this. "Oh geez, that sounds as corny as Raahi's explanation, doesn't it?"

"Do you believe us?" Raahi said.

Jigme gulped. "Can you prove it?"

"I don't see why we need to," Raahi said. "You *must* help us. It is the will of the gods."

"No it isn't, don't listen to him," Kate said. "He's just full of himself. Listen, our guides, the yaks, brought us to you so they must want you to help us. *Can* you help us?"

Jigme frowned. "I'll try. But help you with what?"

<<<>>>

SABURO STOOD SILENT, listening to the other kids speak. He fingered the golden object in his hand, feeling frustrated. Kate still held her lipstick tube so he understood what she said. His English was getting better, and he understood most words, but not all. He sidled closer to Kate.

"*Should* we ask for his help?"

"Do *you* know anything about Bhutan? I've never even heard of this country. We don't know what demon we're searching for and we don't know where to go. Our guides might know, but they can't talk to us or explain what to do. This kid could help."

"Raahi seems to know about Bhutan," Saburo said. "Maybe he knows what we're supposed to do."

Kate made a face. "I don't trust that kid. He has shifty eyes. I'd trust the new kid more than I'd trust Raahi."

Saburo nodded. He didn't like Raahi any more than Kate. The new boy, Jigme, seemed nice enough. Saburo stepped forward and held out his hand.

"Do you know what that is?" Kate said, nodding towards the golden object.

"Of course," Jigme said. "It's a *dorje*. We have one in our shrine at the farmhouse."

"Yeah, but this one is special. We need it to defeat a demon. What kind of demons do you got here in Bhutan?"

Jigme frowned. "The normal kinds, I guess. If you believe in that sort of thing."

"Well, we do. We've fought demons before. Got any local ones you know about? We were dropped into this valley for a reason, I'm guessing."

"Why do you need to fight demons?"

Kate shrugged. "Because we're good at it. Well, I don't know about Raahi, but me and Saburo have fought demons before. Anyway, the sun goddess of Japan asked us to do this. So, we're doing it."

She said this so matter-of-factly, as if talking to spirits and fighting demons were a normal occurrence. Saburo glanced at Jigme, wondering if he would accept her statement. Here the poor kid was, heading home after a nice, quiet afternoon, and suddenly strange kids embroiled him in a demon hunt. Well, Saburo knew what *that* felt like.

"I don't know of any demons in the valley," Jigme said, "but one once lived in the mountains." He pointed to the tall peaks running along the valley's edge.

Raahi perked up. "What kind of demon?"

"Well," Jigme said, "the Dochula Pass is up on that mountain. It's the only way to cross over from here to Thimphu, the capital. A demoness used to guard the pass, but the Divine Madman fought and conquered her."

"The who?"

"The Divine Madman. His real name was Drukpa Kuenley and he was a monk who came here from Tibet. His temple is right there on the hill." Jigme pointed to the temple the young boy monks had marched into for their daily lessons.

"But he already conquered the demon?" Raahi said.

"That's how the story goes."

"How long ago?" Kate asked.

"Six hundred years," Jigme said. "A long time ago."

Saburo gazed across the valley. A dented truck chugged up the dirt road. "Look, they have cars. We aren't back in time. How are we supposed to fight a demon that somebody already conquered centuries ago?"

Kate glanced at the setting sun. "Well, we aren't going to figure it out before dark falls, that's for sure. Jigme, got a place we can hole up for the night?"

Raahi glowered as he stared at his new bedroom. "This is absolutely unacceptable."

Kate snuggled down in the thick hay. "Get off your high horse, Raahi. You won't die if you have to sleep in a stable one night."

Jigme shot one nervous glance at the farmhouse, wishing it wasn't so close to the barn. In fact, the barn made up the farmhouse's first floor. Jigme's family stored grain on the second floor and lived on the third. It made sense to stack the barn, grainery and house together, but he worried he might get into trouble.

"My parents won't be happy if they find you here so please keep quiet. I'll be back first thing in the morning before my father wakes up," he said. "I hope your yaks don't wander off."

Kate grinned. "They won't. And at least they can eat grass, but what about us? I'm starving. We haven't had anything to eat for hours."

Jigme shuffled through his backpack and pulled out the bag of zaw. "Here. There's a pump right outside the barn where you can get water, but please be quiet."

Kate grabbed a handful of the sweet grain and crunched down. "Mmm, this is yummy. OK, so what's our plan for tomorrow?"

"We head to the Dochula Pass," Saburo said.

"What do we do when we get there?"

Saburo shrugged. "I don't know, but something will happen. It always does."

7

The Three Delusions

JIGME LEFT THEM with the dog and a cow in the next stall, and they huddled against the wall. Raahi moved to the far corner and sulked. Kate and Saburo ignored him. Kate rolled her lipstick tube around in her hand. Sparkles shot from it.

"Can anyone hear me?" Pietro's voice floated through the barn.

Saburo fumbled for his spoon. Kate pulled the tube up to her mouth. "Pietro! I can hear you, but you have to whisper. We don't want anyone to hear us."

"OK. Where are you?"

"We're in Bhutan. It's a country up in the Himalayas, between India, Nepal, and Tibet. Present day, we think."

"And what exactly are you supposed to do there?"

"The usual. Fight a demon. Return a treasure. We aren't sure what demon or what treasure though."

49

Jinjing's voice floated into the room. "Bhutan? I'll do some research."

"We think there's a demoness in a place called Dochula. But our new friend, Jigme, doesn't know too much about it. He said something about a Divine Madman conquering the demoness years ago. But we're in present day. Got any ideas?"

"Yes," Pietro said. "The old legend isn't completely true."

"You know the Divine Madman legend?"

"No, I've never heard it before. But think about it. On our last adventure when we were fighting the Four Fiends, they all had legends connected with them. But the legends weren't totally true. I mean, we had to help the old man in China figure out how to defeat the Nian, the Jersey Devil turned out to be a good guy, Pele was a nutcase, and Pandora was a little kid."

"So how does that help us here?" Saburo said.

"I'm just saying. Just because the legend says some mad guy defeated the demon, it doesn't necessarily mean he did. Maybe he just tamed it or something, and now that he's dead and gone, the demon is still lurking about up there. Anyway, how's the new kid doing?"

Saburo brought his voice down to a whisper. He knew Raahi couldn't understand his Japanese. "We don't like him. He thinks he's a god. He complains about everything. I wish you and Jinjing were here."

"I wish we were too," Pietro said. "I have a test tomorrow and I don't want to study for it."

"It's not fair that you guys got to go and we didn't," Jinjing said. "But maybe there's a reason."

"Like what?" Pietro said.

"Well, last time, we had more information to go on. I mean, the Yellow Dragon told us a little about what we had to do. But this time, all Kate and Saburo know is that they have to fight three demons and get three treasures. But no hint as to what the demons are or how they're supposed to defeat them. They don't even have any magical weapons."

"We've got the three Japanese spirits," Saburo said. "So far, they've only acted as our transports, but they're powerful spirits. They can turn into anything, and Amaterasu said they'd provide all that we needed."

Kate chewed on her zaw. "They sure have been scanty on providing food. Thank God Jigme gave us this crunchy stuff. It tastes really good, but it isn't gonna last long."

Saburo grinned. "Not the way you're going through it. Save some for us."

"Can't help it. It's addictive as anything."

"Listen," Jinjing said. "Do either of you have a watch?"

"Nope," Kate said. "I just use my cell phone to check the time, but it's dead now."

"Raahi has a watch," Saburo said. "What time does your watch say, Raahi?"

Raahi glowered at him before glancing at his watch. "It's eight o'clock at night. In Deshnoke, anyway."

"Hold on, I'll look up time zones," Jinjing said. They waited, then she said, "Thimphu is a half hour past Deshnoke so it'll be eight-thirty there. And that matches up with my time here in Hong Kong. It's ten-thirty at night here. And it should be, let's see, four in the afternoon in Italy. Am I right, Pietro?"

"You're right," Pietro said.

"So we're all in the right time zones. Which means we must be in the present," Saburo said.

"That's what I think," Jinjing said. "Listen, everyone have their magical objects handy in exactly two hours from now. I'm thinking the best way to figure out what you guys should do is for Pietro and me to find out as much information as we can on our computers. Then we'll let you know what we find out."

"Sounds like a plan," Pietro said. "Let's meet back in two hours."

SABURO YAWNED AND opened his eyes. The sun shone through the cracks between the boards, coating half the stall in sunlight and half in shadow. In the corner, Raahi snored next to his bakeneko. Tanuki licked Kate's face, trying to wake her.

"Ew. Off, Tanuki." She sat up and untangled hay from her hair. In the stall's doorway, Jigme stood with a tea tray, staring with wide eyes.

"Where did *they* come from?" he whispered, nodding at the animals snuggled in the hay.

"Oh, them," Kate said, pushing Tanuki as far away from her as she could. "Those *were* our yaks."

Jigme managed to put down the tray without spilling the tea. "I brought you some breakfast.

My parents will be up soon so you'll have to leave before they see you."

Kate shook Raahi awake and they all drank the sweet, creamy tea. "This is great. What is it?" Kate asked.

"Butter tea."

"Why's it called that?"

"Because it has yak and cow butter in it. You can put some zaw in the tea and soften it. It tastes good that way."

He passed around slices of dry toast topped with butter. "That's all I could sneak out. Did you find out anything new?"

Kate nodded. "Do you know anything about the Three Poisonous Delusions?"

Jigme shook his head.

"It's a Buddhist thing, apparently. Jinjing looked it up. She thinks they might be the demons we have to fight. The first is desire, the second is hatred, and the third is...oh drat, I forget."

Raahi yawned. "Closed-mindedness."

"Yeah, that. See, last time we took one of these journeys, we had to fight demons that possessed traits we had. Like I had to fight gluttony, and Saburo had to fight chaos because we fought with those things in our normal lives too."

Jigme nodded, trying to understand. Raahi sipped his tea and listened, intrigued. "*You* were a glutton?"

Kate nodded. "Not a glutton in the sense that I ate a lot. But I wanted everything to go my way."

Raahi frowned. "That doesn't sound like gluttony to me."

"I know, but you have to loosely interpret these things. Anyway, Pietro thinks we each have one of these traits. Desire, hatred, and closed-mindedness. The Three Poisonous Delusions."

"The first demon to fight is mine," Saburo said, gripping the golden dorje in his hand. "But I do not know which one it is."

"You don't hate," Kate said, "so I bet you don't have to fight that. Are you close-minded?"

Saburo shrugged. "I don't know."

"How 'bout desire? Got any of that?"

Saburo gulped. He wasn't about to tell Kate he found *her* desirable. The heat rose in his face.

"Well," Kate said, "it doesn't matter. We'll figure it out when we get to the Dochula Pass. I guess we'd better go."

The kitsune picked her way through the hay, her six tails fanning out behind her. The delicate creature stopped in front of Jigme and stared at him with her emerald eyes. He blinked.

"I must go too."

"You must?" Kate said.

Jigme nodded. "Your fox told me so."

"We don't need another person," Raahi said. "We don't have an animal for you to ride."

"Quiet, boy," Kate said. "We didn't need you either, but we're stuck with you, aren't we? If the fox says Jigme should come, Jigme'll come. He can ride with me."

"Or me," Saburo said, not liking the thought of Jigme riding so close to Kate.

Jigme took a deep breath. He looked nervous. "It's a long way up to the pass. I'm glad we don't have to walk."

8

The Bird

JIGME GLANCED OVER his shoulder. Behind him, Raahi sat with a sour look on his face and stared at the swirly black and white hairs on his yak's back.

"You're supposed to be my magical creature," Raahi said to the yak. "You should obey my command. I want to go first. I want to head this adventure."

But the yak shook its ears and plodded behind the others. Raahi looked over the mountainside. He didn't gasp with awe at the beautiful valley below, he didn't sigh with contentment as he breathed the fresh air. Jigme decided the boy must hate this place, and he had the suspicion that Raahi didn't much like these kids who refused to give him the respect he thought he deserved. Jigme felt sad for him. The others oohed and aahed at the beautiful rhododen-drons spilling down the mountainside, and Kate, who sat in front of him on the Tanuki-yak, whooped with happiness. She watched an eagle swirl overhead.

"It's huge!" she yelled. "You sure have big birds here, Jigme."

Jigme gazed up at it, and his heart, which had already had quite a bit of a shock today, started thumping against his ribs. "No we don't. I've never seen a bird that big. How can it even fly?"

Saburo's yak trotted out in front, picking its way over the rocks. Kate's Tanuki-yak stumbled over practically every stone in its path. "Sorry, Jigme," she said.

"It's OK," Jigme said. Kate had told him that he couldn't fall off, but every time Tanuki took a stumble, he wanted to grab hold of her just in case. The fact that she was a girl stopped him. He didn't want her to take his grabbing the wrong way.

Kate spoke into her lipstick tube. "Saburo, can you hear me?"

Saburo's muffled voice answered her. "I hear you, Kate."

Jigme marveled at the tube. "It translates what he's saying," he said.

"You can hear that?" Kate turned half around and flashed her deep blue eyes at him. He gulped.

"Of course. Why?"

"Raahi can't understand anything coming from the tube, that's all. I wonder why you can." She turned back around. "Saburo, Jigme's never seen a bird that big. You think maybe it's not a bird?"

"What else would it be?"

"I dunno. We're getting close to the pass, right? Maybe it's the demon thingy."

"Or the demon's spy," Jigme put in.

The eagle circled lower. Its huge talons curled beneath it, and it glared at them with fiery eyes.

"Yep, definitely a demon. Real eagles don't have red eyes." Kate prodded Tanuki. "Catch up with Saburo, why don't you, you lazy animal? That bird is about to dive and pluck us right off your back."

Tanuki grunted and shuffled a little faster.

"Well, would ya look at that. He's actually doing what I asked for once," Kate said.

Jigme gulped, trying to get some moisture into his throat. "It's staring at me."

"The bird?"

"Yes. It won't stop staring at me. Look at those claws. And that beak."

"You're safe with Tanuki," Kate said.

The eagle swooped lower. Jigme marveled at its massive size.

"What do you think it wants?" Kate said.

"It wants me. I shouldn't have come."

"Jigme, you're being paranoid. Why would the bird single you out? You're more or less our guide, I guess, but you don't have to fight the demoness. Saburo does."

Jigme couldn't slow his pounding heart. His eyes locked onto the soaring eagle. "I don't care. He won't stop looking at me, Kate."

The eagle screamed. Its whistle blasted through the trees and stung Jigme's ears. Tanuki stopped and reared.

"Hold on!" Kate said, but he couldn't. He slipped off the animal's back and landed in soft grass. Kate fell on top of him.

"Sorry," she said, rolling off.

Jigme didn't even notice. He watched, mesmerized. The raccoon dog-yak rose on its back legs. The brown yak hair shortened.

"What's happening?" he whispered.

Kate watched Tanuki. "He's shape-shifting. Wow."

The yak's hooves morphed into large paws with sharp claws. The thin legs widened into thick stumps. Tanuki roared. His blast drowned out the eagle's screams.

Jigme gasped. "It's a bear. Your yak is a bear."

"Well, now he is." Kate said.

The eagle headed toward them in a tight dive. The bear swiped a huge claw into the air and swatted the bird away like it was smacking a volleyball. The bird screamed, flapping its wings to steady itself.

"Go Tanuki!" Saburo yelled, scrambling over to hunker with Kate and Jigme.

"Where's Kitsune?" Kate said.

Saburo grinned. "Look up."

A huge red bird streaked after the eagle. "Hey, that's the Vermillion Bird!" Kate said.

"The what?" Raahi asked, crawling over to join them.

"The bird I saved on our last adventure."

"It's not, it's Kitsune," Saburo said.

Kitsune didn't wait for the eagle to right itself. She dove, wings beating, beak snapping and claws slashing. The eagle didn't have a chance. It fell.

Bakeneko bounded after it. She had changed back to her cat shape, but had grown to an enormous size, larger than a tiger. She leaped down the mountainside and disappeared between the trees. A scream echoed up the mountain (the eagle) and a hiss. Bakeneko, Jigme guessed.

"Looks like the eagle's done for," Raahi said. His grin looked evil, like he was enjoying this. Jigme felt sorry for the eagle, but he was still glad it was gone.

"Poor thing," Kate said.

Jigme shuddered. "Poor thing? It was about to eat me."

"How do you know it was going for you? I was right next to you. It could've been after me."

"No, it stared right at me. I don't like this. I want to go home."

Kate reached back and gave the boy's shoulder a sympathetic pat. It didn't help much. He hadn't asked to get thrown into this mess. If he hadn't gone down to the river that afternoon, he might not have gotten mixed up in all this.

"Sorry, you can't go home," Kate said. "Not yet. You're stuck with us until this whole adventure is over and done with. That's how it works."

"Why am I here? Why did your fox want me to come too? You don't need me. Your magical creatures could've found this place without me pointing out the way. I'm not needed here."

"You are," Kate said, "even if we don't know why yet. The kitsune must have her reason. You'll just have to trust her."

Raahi frowned. "I want to know who sent the eagle."

"Maybe the eagle was the demon," Kate said.

Raahi shook his head. "No. The demon wouldn't come out herself. She'd send scouts first."

Jigme forgot his fear. He turned to the Indian boy. "Why would she do that?"

Raahi shrugged. "That's what I would do."

Jigme scrutinized the boy. He'd bet anything that not only would Raahi do it, he probably already had. Jigme had met up with bullies before and he could tell Raahi was a bully. If Raahi found a new kid he wanted to torment, his larger friends probably scouted the victim out first. Found out the kid's weaknesses. Then Raahi would step in.

Jigme wondered why such a spiteful boy would be sent on such an important quest. He turned to Tanuki, still in bear form, busy scratching his rear end with one hairy paw. Kate followed Jigme's gaze and grinned.

"Thanks for saving us, Tanuki," she said. "You're not so bad."

Kitsune flitted to the ground and Bakeneko lumbered up the slope. "I wish they could talk," Kate said. "I'm sure they know more about this adventure than they can tell us."

"If Jinjing were here," Saburo said, "she'd think this through. Remember how she figured out the Four Guardians and the Four Fiends?"

"But she knew about them already. We don't know anything about the Three...oh, I forget what they are already."

"The Three Poisonous Delusions," Raahi said. "Hate, desire, and closed-mindedness."

"Right that. See, I can't remember them. But at least you know about the Three Treasures, Saburo. Do they have any specific qualities?"

Saburo frowned. "I don't know. I'm not as good at history as Jinjing. She'd know. All I do know about the Three Treasures is that they're the Emperor's divine symbols. Oh, and I think there's some symbolism in there somewhere. The sword represents the stars, and the mirror is the sun, and the jewel is the moon. I think. But that's all I know."

He pulled the golden dorje from his pocket. "And all we have to fight the demon with is that," Kate said. "I wonder what it does."

"It's the scepter of Buddha," Jigme said.

"What's a scepter?" Kate said.

Jigme shrugged. "Something a great person holds, to show their importance." He held out his hand. Saburo hesitated before dropping the dorje into the boy's outstretched palm.

"You see, the dorje is symmetrical. The center here is shaped like a ball, representing the center of the universe. Energy flows from it to the two ends. The ends are shaped like five arms that come together; see, they are like sunrays and they meet at the ends."

Kate peered over his shoulder. "What does it all mean though?"

Jigme thought hard about his lessons. If he were like the boy monks, he would know all this by now, but he never excelled at studying. He liked to read, but not so much to learn as to escape to a new world and place. His family was Buddhist, but he did not know much about it himself.

He wracked his brains, trying to remember everything he could about the dorje. This was important. This must be why he was here—so he could explain the dorje to these kids. He wondered why the magical creatures hadn't picked a child monk from the temple to help them instead. A monk would understand this stuff.

"The five rays come together at the end to symbolize your entire life experience," he said. "Each ray stands for something different, something you're supposed to learn during your lifetime. Oh bother."

The others waited patiently while he thought. He closed his eyes and tried to remember his lessons. "Wisdom. They represent different types of wisdom. But I can't remember what the types are." He shook his head, frustrated.

Kitsune crawled to him. She had turned back into a fox. She licked his face and curled up next to him. Jigme patted her head.

And then, he remembered one.

"Wisdom of the Great Mirror."

Saburo sucked in his breath. "What?"

"The Great Mirror. Wisdom of the Great Mirror. I can't remember what it means, but that's one of the Wisdoms."

"The same as the mirror we're trying to find?" Kate said.

"I don't know."

Kate and Saburo glanced at each other. "What symbols are associated with the mirror again?" Kate asked.

Saburo shook his head. "I can't remember."

"The sun," Raahi said.

Saburo frowned. It must be annoying for him, Jigme thought, Raahi remembering all the facts when Saburo couldn't.

Saburo sighed. "I can never remember my history." Kitsune moved to him and licked his hand. His eyes suddenly shone.

"Oh, I've got it! *Yata no Kogami*, that's the mirror's name. It represents wisdom."

"Like Jigme's Buddhist mirror," Kate said.

"And, it also represents honesty."

Kate nodded. "OK. So, we've got some stuff to work with here. Honesty, wisdom, and the sun. That's what the mirror is all about. And Saburo's got the dorje to fight the demoness."

"How do you think that'll work?" Saburo asked, taking the dorje back from the Jigme.

An eerie wind rustled through the trees, sending shivers down Jigme's spine. He stood, nervous and alert. Mixed in with the wind floated a high, piercing scream.

Jigme gulped. "I don't know, but I think we're about to find out."

9

The Dochula Pass

Raahi put his hands over his ears. "Someone shut that noise up. Please!"

Kate glared at him. "Oh sure, right away Your Highness." She turned to Saburo. "What do you think it is?"

Saburo shook his head, cringing. Kate turned to Jigme. "What is the demoness like? The one the Divine Madman fought?"

Jigme shook his head too. "I don't know. She's just a demoness. I've never seen a picture of her. And he didn't really fight her. He…"

Saburo perked up his ears. Maybe Jigme could tell them how the Madman had conquered the demoness, and then he could do the same.

"He got her to fall in love with him, I think," Jigme said, his face turning red.

"What?" Saburo said.

Kate laughed and talked into her lipstick tube so Saburo could understand. "Oh," he said. "Well, *that* isn't going to happen."

"Make it stop," Raahi moaned again, pushing his hands tight against his ears.

"We can't, so quit whining," Kate said.

Saburo sat up and uncovered his ears. He had to prepare himself. He glanced at the guardians. They had their eyes trained towards the distant scream. Tanuki's bear form morphed into the yak.

"C'mon," Kate said, yanking Raahi to his feet. "We're moving."

"I don't want to," Raahi said, keeping his hands clamped to his ears. "I can't stand that sound."

"Good thing you don't have to fight it then," Kate said. "You'd be useless. Get on Bakeneko. We've gotta go."

Saburo didn't want to head towards the sound either, but he was ready to face it. He had fought a cyclone demon once, riding on the Jersey Devil's back, and knew he had the strength to face another demon if he had to. He trusted Kitsune. She would protect him from any harm.

But what did he have to do? The dorje was hot in his hand, as if it were warming up, getting ready. He gripped it. Its warmth flooded into him, and he felt strong. Confident. Whatever lay ahead, he would be ready for it.

Saburo straightened on his yak. Immediately, as if his strength acted like a magnet, Kate sat up too. So did Jigme behind her. Saburo's confidence was contagious. He glanced at Raahi, who had his eyes shut as he slumped over his yak.

"This is all a dream," Raahi murmured. "I'm back at home with my father and I'll wake up soon."

"No you won't," Kate said. "Get a grip, Raahi."

The yaks broke into a gallop, tearing up the path until they reached the main road. Up until that point, Saburo had forgotten they weren't in some distant past. They were here, in the real world, and vehicles choked the road they galloped up now.

The vehicles had all screeched to a crazy stop. The drivers could hear the inhuman noise too. Up ahead, two trucks had smashed into each other. One hung half off the cliff edge.

The yaks leaped over the trucks and kept going. Saburo gripped his magical spoon. Above the piercing screams, he could hear Kate whooping.

"I know I should be terrified, but that was fun! I hope those drivers are OK. Are you all right up there, Saburo?"

"Fine. Just trying to figure out what to do."

"Don't worry about it too much. It'll come to you, it always does."

Yes, but this is a different adventure, Saburo thought. What if things work differently here? He felt so unprepared. As they raced forward, he tried to think, tried to put the pieces together.

He had to fight a demon. And he'd have to face either hatred, desire or closed-mindedness. He had the dorje. He still didn't know what weapon it would turn into, but it contained wisdom, he knew that. Maybe it would give him the wisdom he needed to fight the demon. But besides the dorje, he didn't have a weapon to fight the demon with.

Which poisonous delusion must he face? He felt like he possessed all three.

But…what had he felt when he first got pulled into this adventure? Hatred. Hatred towards his dead father, and his father's new family. That emotion coursed through him when Kitsune found him wandering through the back alley.

The piercing scream strengthened, but Saburo didn't hear it anymore. His mind cleared. Focused. He knew what he had to fight. He wasn't sure how he would fight it, but he must clear his mind of all hatred. And that started with his father.

His mother had never talked much about his father. Saburo remembered his two small step-brothers at the funeral, crying for their loss. Taro had been sad too. They all loved their father. So he couldn't have been a bad person.

But why had he never visited? Why had he just walked away and forgotten about his original sons? Saburo remembered how his mother would always gloss over the subject. Tell him not to think about it. He loved his mother. But maybe she shared the blame. Maybe she hadn't *wanted* his father to keep in touch.

No, that didn't help. Now he felt a little hatred for his mother too. He *had* to come to terms with this. And he had to do it soon.

Kate's voice echoed from the spoon. "Jigme says we're getting close to the Dochula Pass."

Saburo's yak jumped over another car and swerved around two men standing in the road, their ears covered and their mouths hanging open as they stared towards the pass. He took a deep breath. The closer they got, the calmer he felt. He gripped the dorje and watched it glow.

"Whatever it is, it's coming up," he said into his spoon.

<<<>>>

JIGME KEPT HIS eyes trained on the road. A hill loomed ahead. Several square white buildings with brown roofs covered it.

"What's that?" Kate asked.

"Those are the Chortens," Jigme said. "They were erected a few years ago, in honor of His Majesty the King. We're at the Dochula Pass."

Tourist buses clustered around the Chortens, but all the tourists were flooding down the hill and away from the white buildings, screaming. The yaks charged up the rocky steps winding around the small buildings. A larger white structure stood at the top

Perched on its roof, her eyes blazing and her mouth open in a constant scream, stood the Demoness of Dochula Pass.

The yaks stopped. Kate gulped. "Holy cow."

The demoness's red robes flowed like fire; writhing snakes adorned her head. A long, forked tongue poked out of a mouth lined with jagged teeth. In one hand she held a spear, in the other a round shield.

Kate turned to Jigme. "The Divine Madman fell in love with *that* thing?"

Jigme shuddered and hid behind Kate. "I don't even want to look at her." He glanced to where Raahi's yak stood. The boy had his arms wrapped around his head and his face buried in Bakeneko's neck.

"Well, you're doing better than Raahi, the big baby," Kate said. "Saburo, what do we do now?"

"I don't know."

Even with this admission, Saburo's voice sounded calm. Jigme watched him, wondering what he'd do. Saburo gripped the dorje, which now glowed like a flashlight. The demoness turned her fiery eyes towards him and raised her spear.

Jigme gulped, watching in horror. Saburo had only the dorje to protect himself. And Kitsune.

The fox reared and Saburo slid off. He landed on his feet, looking steady and determined. As the demoness flung her spear, the fox leaped into the air and morphed into a wispy, silver light. The spear penetrated the light and turned to dust, which fell to the earth, useless. The demoness screamed and jumped from the building to the ground, enraged.

As Kitsune reshaped, Tanuki the Bear charged. He barreled into the demoness, but only hit the white building's side; the demoness had vanished but reappeared behind them. Saburo spun around as she hissed.

Kate kicked Raahi, who had been dumped by Bakeneko and had curled himself into a ball. "Get up, boy. Make yourself useful."

"Useful to do what?" Jigme whispered, still hiding behind her. "What can we do against something that can disappear and reappear like that?"

10

The Mirror

ALL HIS LIFE, Saburo's mother had been alone. His father had left right before Saburo's birth. Saburo's mother never talked about his father. Ever. When he was little, he asked his mother and brothers about his father, mostly due to curiosity. His father didn't seem like a real person; Saburo pictured him more as a nondescript figure wandering out there somewhere. He never could put a face to the man, or a voice, or an emotion.

But when Saburo turned nine, his older brother Taro took a trip to Tokyo and came back with presents from their father.

"I don't think these presents are really from him," Jiro whispered to Saburo. "I think Taro bought them and is pretending like our father sent them. He doesn't really care about us."

Jiro was at the stage where everything angered him, and he loathed their father. Since Taro or his mother rarely spoke of the man, Saburo believed what Jiro said. By the time his father passed away, Saburo truly believed he was a mean, cruel monster, and their lives had been better off without him.

Now he realized that probably wasn't true.

The demoness reappeared, hissing and snarling on the hill's other side. She scooted around a building. Saburo glanced past her, to the parking lot where a crowd hunkered behind the tour buses, watching the action.

Kitsune came to him and licked his face. He understood. Now was the time for him to confront the demoness. The Japanese spirits would help, but they could not regain the mirror. He must do it himself.

He walked steadily towards the building the demoness had ducked behind. He gripped the dorje. It still glowed in his hand. "What do I have to do?" he whispered to Kitsune.

The fox opened her mouth.

"Saburo."

Saburo jumped. Hearing a human voice echoing from Kitsune's mouth scared him ten times worse than listening to the demoness hissing behind her white building. The deep, friendly voice belong to a man.

"Kitsune?"

"No. You don't know who this is?"

Saburo gulped. He knew.

"Oto-san?"

"Yes."

Was Kitsune playing tricks on him? Or was he really hearing his father, his *oto-san*?

"You're dead," Saburo whispered.

"I am a spirit now. Your spirit guide can communicate with me."

Too creepy. Saburo gripped the dorje. He'd rather face the demoness than have this conversation. But Kitsune hadn't channeled his father's spirit at this moment for no reason.

He waited. He expected maybe an apology, a reason as to why his father had missed his childhood, had been so distant. But the voice said none of these things. Instead it said, "Do you trust me?"

Anger welled up in Saburo's chest. *No. Why should I trust you? A man I don't even know?*

"I trust Kitsune," he said.

"You must trust me, Saburo. I will not steer you wrong."

Saburo gripped the dorje, seething.

<<<>>>

RAAHI SIDLED OVER to Jigme. "What's happening?"

"I don't know. Saburo is just standing there, staring at the fox. They aren't doing anything."

"Where's the demoness?"

"Behind the chorten. She's not doing anything either."

"If she were smart," Raahi said, "she'd pounce now when Saburo isn't ready."

"Say that a little louder, why don't you?" Kate hissed. "Let that demon hear you. I'm sure she'd *love* to take your advice."

74

She was being sarcastic, but watching Raahi, Jigme wondered if the boy might actually do just that. Raahi obviously didn't like Saburo much. He didn't like the superior-sounding Kate either. In fact, the Indian boy didn't seem to get along with *anybody.*

Jigme's eyes refocused on Saburo, who was obviously wrestling with some inner demon. He tapped Kate on her shoulder. "Look at his hand."

Kate looked. The golden dorje, which had been so luminescent earlier, had faded to a dull yellow. "I don't get it," she said. "What's happening to the dorje?"

"Remember what I said about the five rays? They were like rays of sunlight, of wisdom. Earlier, they were bright. Now they're dimming. I think they mirror what Saburo is feeling. He had confidence earlier. Now, not so much."

Kate turned to Tanuki. "Can we help him?"

The dog-bear answered by shuffling forward, blocking any chance of approaching Saburo and giving him some aid. So, Kate yelled instead.

"Saburo! Look at the dorje!"

SABURO GLANCED AT the dull metal lying in his hand. Where had the light gone?

The fox's mouth opened wider. "Saburo. You must trust me."

Must trust? Why? What had his father ever done for him, except ignore him? He shut his eyes, remembering the white bones lying on that sterile tray. He shuddered, but he also remembered his half-brother's tear-streaked faces.

They had loved him. Loved the father Saburo never knew. Saburo still didn't feel any love, but a strange compassion for those two little boys grew in his heart. His jealousy melted as he remembered their pain and sorrow. He realized his hatred had been no more than jealousy for a love they enjoyed and he could never have.

He opened his eyes, gripped the dorje tight in his fist, and took a deep, shaky breath. "I trust you. I may not know you, but I will trust you, Oto-san."

"Good," his father said. "Then this is what you must do."

JIGME COVERED HIS ears. The demoness had resumed her screaming. The sound frightened him, but not as much as it terrified Raahi. That boy fell to the ground and curled in a ball, his hands clamped over his ears.

And Saburo just stood there, still as a statue. "Why doesn't he *do* something?" Jigme whispered.

"He *is* doing something," Kate said. "He's thinking. Geez, Raahi, get up. You must have super-sensitive hearing if the screams bug you that much." She folded her arms, keeping them away from her ears to stress her point.

Raahi didn't answer. Jigme knew how the boy felt. It wasn't the scream, or its shrillness. It was the fear. Every time the demoness opened her mouth, Raahi cringed and moaned. His body trembled and his legs shook.

Jigme wondered why that unearthly voice didn't affect him the same way. He was afraid, but Saburo and Kate stood calm and in control. Their surety that everything would turn out all right comforted him.

<<◇>>

SABURO STILL STOOD, waiting. He scrutinized the gawking group of tourists huddled around the buses. It annoyed him that they were content to watch but not help.

The demoness sprung. With no warning, she catapulted over the building. Saburo sprinted as fast as his bad leg would allow. He managed to move out of her way, but he stumbled and smashed to the ground as the demoness skidded past him.

"Saburo!" Kate yelled.

Saburo whipped his head around. The demoness charged the three other kids. Kate stood resolute but a little shaky, Jigme cowered behind her, and Raahi writhed on the ground, his hands clamped against his ears, tears streaming down his face.

The three guardians leapt into action. They morphed into tigers. Kitsune swished her six tails and roared at the demoness, her red stripes blazing. Bakeneko's swirly-striped body towered over the demoness, her teeth a row of jagged daggers. Fat, bumbly Tanuki sprang forward, blocking Kate and gnashing at the demon. All his roly-polyness vanished as a sleek, brown tiger with sharp claws took his place.

The demoness's scream turned into a frightened wail. She backed away and held up her shield. From behind her, Saburo watched as the shield's shiny, polished surface winked at him.

It wasn't a shield at all. It was the mirror.

Saburo thought back to a book his mother owned on Japanese mythology. That book showed the sword, the jewel, and the mirror. The round brass mirror looked like a shield. But it was polished so bright, Saburo could see his reflection in it.

"*Yata no kagami,*" he said, grinning. "There you are."

He raised his hand.

The demoness spun toward him. She had forgotten him and the dorje he held, but she now spotted him in the mirror. A high, hissing sound burst from her blood-red mouth. The others, even Kate, covered their ears. Only Saburo heard the words.

You think you have me, boy. But look at what you hold. You don't even know how to wield it.

"I do," Saburo said, gripping the dorje so tight his hand hurt. "*This* will stop you."

The demoness's laughing voice crackled into the sky. Saburo could hear the tourists scream as hot, white sparks burst like repulsive fireworks over the Chortens.

Saburo dared to take his eyes off the evil creature and glance at the dorje. It barely glowed. Why? He had done what his father asked. He had put aside his hatred.

But did he believe it?

Saburo grimaced. Why did he have to concentrate on this now? If he wanted to feed power into the dorje, he must find peace. But how could he be peaceful while the demoness screamed and shot sparks in to the air, his friends cowered on the ground, and he had to concentrate?

Maybe you don't have to concentrate. Maybe you just have to let go.

Kitsune sprang between Saburo and the demoness. She screamed but didn't dare get near the tigers circling her. Saburo wished they'd jump on her and finish her off, but that wasn't how the game was played. The only way to defeat the demoness was to use the dorje. And the only way to use the dorje was to be at peace.

Let go. Let him go. And as the thought raced through Saburo's mind, he realized maybe he wasn't angry at his father. Not really. He was angry at himself. He wanted his father. But maybe that wasn't what his father needed. Maybe he truly belonged with his second family.

But Saburo hadn't wanted to accept that. His brother Taro, who knew his father best, had accepted it. Saburo, who had never even met his father, couldn't.

"I wanted you," he whispered. "I wanted a father."

He knew now that could never be. It hurt, but he had to live with that knowledge and move on.

The dorje's glow got stronger. Kitsune padded out of the way, and the demoness towered over him. The tigers boxed her in on her other three sides, but now he stood in her direct target line.

He grabbed his spoon. "Kate," he said. "Distract the demon."

"How? She doesn't want me. She's totally after you."

"I need her to turn around. She's got the mirror's dull side facing me, and I need the shiny side. Trust me."

The demoness moved towards him, the grass burning under her feet. She raised the mirror.

79

A huge, deafening blast echoed across the hill. Its force flung Saburo backwards, and the demoness spun around to face this new threat.

Saburo couldn't help laughing. Tanuki had morphed into a huge brown elephant. His nose stuck straight into the sky as he trumpeted his rage. From below, the tourists began screaming all over again and dove to take shelter behind their buses.

The elephant was all bluff of course, but that didn't matter. With her back turned, Saburo could see the mirror glinting in the sunlight. He closed his eyes for a moment and smiled.

"Good-bye, Oto-san."

He raised his hand. A blinding white light shot from the dorje and smashed into the mirror, refracting into a million rays. The demoness let out an ear-splitting shriek and exploded. The shockwave sent Saburo reeling halfway down the hill. He landed against something soft.

Kitsune's six tails wrapped around him, cushioning him to the ground. He watched as the sky burst with fire and light.

"Is she gone?"

Kitsune let out a low yowl.

"And the mirror? It's not destroyed, is it?"

"Saburo!" Kate yelled. She ran towards him, a wild grin on her face. He tried to get up, but she tackled him to the ground and hugged him. Saburo knew his face must be bright red by now.

"That was awesome," Kate said. "And you're still in one piece."

Saburo laughed. "We did it. Thanks Kate."

"For what?"

"For getting Tanuki to help."

"Oh that." She grinned. "He isn't so bad. He's slow and bumbly and needs a good bath, but he comes through when ya need him. Let's get the mirror and get outta here before the cops show up. We're attracting a crowd."

Saburo watched the tourists scramble into their buses. A fire truck howled around the bend, and it wouldn't be long before people would storm up the hill to find out what had happened. He turned his eyes towards the mirror. Raahi held it in his hands, staring at it.

"Hand it over, boy," Kate said, making a grab for it, but Raahi yanked it away.

"It belongs to me. I picked it up."

"Like poop it does. All you did was cower on the ground with your hands over your ears. Saburo fought the demoness, I helped, and Jigme, well, he didn't do much but at least he didn't act like a weenie baby."

"That was amazing," Jigme said, joining them. His eyes were so round, he looked like a cartoon character. "But Kate is right. I didn't do much."

Saburo smiled and handed him the still glowing dorje.

"For...for me?" Jigme held up the golden object.

"Careful, Jigme, your eyes are gonna pop right out of their sockets," Kate said. "You might as well keep it. We won't need it anymore. We just need to take the mirror back. And you can't have it," she said to Raahi, who gave her an annoyed pout. "It belongs to the Sun Goddess. Don't think for a minute you're more powerful than she is even if you are Ganesh. Which you're not."

She yanked the mirror from his hands and gave it to Saburo.

<<<>>>

THEY CLIMBED ABOARD their guardians, who had once more changed into lumbering yaks, and trotted down the hill away from the advancing firemen.

"I don't get one thing," Kate said.

"What's that?" Jigme, who bounced behind her, asked.

"The demoness. Those tigers scared the poop outta her. She wasn't afraid of the spirits when they were yaks or when they were elephants or bears, but the tigers totally petrified her. Why?"

Jigme thought. "Well, the Divine Madman once befriended a flying tiger. Maybe the demoness and the tiger were mortal enemies. Maybe that's why she's afraid of tigers."

Kate laughed. "The Madman left her for a tiger, huh? I wonder if the tiger was female."

Jigme laughed too. "Knowing the Divine Madman, probably so."

"Too bad we didn't meet up with this Madman guy. He coulda helped us with the demoness."

"Maybe," Jigme said, "but I think we did just fine on our own."

He suddenly was glad that he met these strange travellers. He'd have one heck of an adventure to tell his friends at school. He wondered if anyone would believe his incredible story.

II

Tsukuyomi

"SOMETHING WEIRD IS going on here," Pietro said.

Kate laughed. "It's always weird, Pietro."

"Not like this. This is totally different than the last adventure if you think about it."

"How is it any different?" Saburo said. "We were sent on a quest to defeat a demon and recapture a prize. And we had to fight down our own fears to do it. It's exactly the same as last time."

"Except there's one big difference. People saw you do it."

Kate frowned. "Come again?"

"You remember the last adventure, right? We went back in time, we weren't in the present day. And not many people except us saw the fiends we were fighting. The old Chinese man, Hongju, saw the Nian. Mrs. Leeds might've spotted the Jersey Devil…"

"Although the Jersey Devil wasn't really the fiend," Saburo said.

"I know, but that's not the point. Then, when we fought the other two fiends, the only people who saw us weren't really people at all. They were gods."

"Pandora," Jinjing said. "She wasn't a god, just a little girl."

"Right, Pandora. But my point is, the people who did see us fight the fiends were people that were somehow already embroiled up in the myths surrounding those creatures. Get it?"

"And now?" Kate said. She tried her best to sound patient although she wished Pietro would get to the point.

"Now, what happened in Bhutan made the news, Kate. I mean, it wasn't huge news, I had to really search for it on the internet, but it *was* news. People are starting to wonder what is going on."

Jinjing's high voice wafted through Kate's lipstick tube. "I agree with Pietro. This is different. It's closer to home."

Pietro went on. "It's like all of a sudden these myths and legends that people only talked about are now becoming more...real. People saw the demoness go up in smoke, they saw the whole light show. I mean, it was in a remote place and there wasn't a huge crowd, but what if it happens again?"

"Does it matter?" Kate said.

"Of course it matters. All throughout history, people have only caught glimpses of these gods and fiends, or whatever you want to call them. They saw enough to make up stories about them. Some were close to the truth, but most were pretty far off, but those occurrences happened rarely. Now, the Demoness of Dochula Pass is making the news."

Kate shrugged. "Might do good for the tourist business in Bhutan."

"Yeah, maybe. But why'd it happen? And will it happen again? Where are you guys now?"

Saburo sat in the soft grass with his back to a rock. On the rock lay the jacket he had discarded yesterday. "We're in the spirit Japan. In Amaterasu's glade. We had to bring the mirror here, but she hasn't shown up yet."

"How long ago did you leave Bhutan?"

"Yesterday afternoon. By the time we got back here it was night. Our guides brought us some food, and we went to sleep. We're just waking up."

"So say about thirteen hours, maybe?"

"Yeah, about that."

"It's been about thirteen hours since your fight with the demoness. The article I found had the time."

"So?" Kate said.

"So," Pietro said, "you're not experiencing any time difference whatsoever. And we're able to talk to you. You're not even in our dimension, you're back in the spirit Japan. But you're so close to us, we can still communicate."

Kate scratched her head and frowned. "But when Saburo fought the demoness, we were in the real world. And now we're back in the spirit world, but I don't even remember how we got here."

"You broke through the plane somehow. You're able to go back and forth, Kate. And so can the spirits."

"But that's happened before," Kate said. "When we fought the Four Fiends, we were in our world, but the spirits were there too."

"But not in our *time*," Pietro said, "and not out in the open. That's the difference."

"WHERE *IS* SHE?" Kate said.

Saburo had moved his coat from the rock and had placed the mirror there. The three guardians had vanished into the woods a few hours ago.

Kate yawned.

Saburo watched her pace around the glade. "Where do you think we'll go next?"

"Who knows?" Kate dropped down beside him. "Why are we doing this, Saburo?"

"Because they need us."

"Who? The gods? Why do they need human kids? Why can't they just send their spirit minions after the demons? I mean, Tanuki is pretty clumsy, but he's not bad in a fight. Why do they need us?"

Raahi looked up from where he sat against a tree, pulling apart grass blades. "I'll tell you why. Because they can't do it themselves."

"Yeah, but why not?"

Raahi shrugged. "Maybe it's easier to get somebody else to do your dirty work for you."

Kate frowned. "We're not doing Amaterasu's dirty work. We're helping her get her treasures back."

"Sounds like dirty work to me. How do you know the treasures belong to her?"

"It's old Japanese mythology. Saburo said so. Right, Saburo?"

Raahi shrugged. "How do you know the old mythology is right? It seems to me, from what you've said before, that mythology is mostly wrong. Humans might have gotten a bit of it right, but not all of it. So, how do we know we're working for the right people?"

Kate laughed. "The other choice is to work for the demons."

"Maybe we should be."

Kate leaned forward. "You mean to tell me you think we should be siding with the demons? The ones who tried to kill us? That demoness would've ripped Saburo's head off if she had a chance."

"So would you if you were being attacked. Never mind if you were good or bad. You'd still fight. How do you know the demoness wasn't just protecting herself?"

"But she had the mirror."

"Who's to say the mirror isn't hers? Maybe Amaterasu stole it. Maybe the demoness was trying to get it back."

Kate glared at the boy. "Maybe you're trying to mess with our minds. Maybe you're a spy for the bad side."

Raahi shrugged. "Well, I never said I'd sign up for your *good* side. I didn't ask to come here at all. As far as I'm concerned, your *good* side kidnapped me. So, I don't see how they're so good."

Kate glanced at Saburo. His eyes were stony. "Do you think Raahi might have a point, Saburo? Do you think we're being used?"

"I don't see that it matters," Saburo said. "We're here. We've been asked to help. So, I will. The sooner we find the other treasures, the sooner we can go home." He locked eyes with Kate. She nodded and broke eye contact as a silver light caught her attention.

The light spread through the glade. A tall man clad in silver robes stepped into the clearing, followed by the three guardians. He approached the rock.

"Tsukiyomi," Saburo whispered. "Get up, Kate."

Kate climbed to her feet and stood next to Saburo. He glared at Raahi, and Raahi reluctantly got up.

"Who is he?" Kate said.

"Tsukiyomi. The moon god. Amaterasu's brother."

"He's handsome," Kate said.

"He's a zillion years old. Stop saying that," Saburo growled.

"Why? You thought the sun goddess was pretty. Why can't I say the moon god is handsome?"

"Just bow," Saburo said, bowing low.

The moon god bowed too. "You have returned the mirror. Thank you."

Kate glanced at Saburo. He stared at the ground. Kate raised her eyes and met Tsukiyomi's.

"What do we have to do now?"

The moon god smiled. "You must recover my sword next. It will be a hard journey. But your spirit guardians will be with you."

"Well, can I ask a question first?"

"Kate!" Saburo hissed. "Quit bothering the god."

"Why? He called us here so he needs us. Seems to me I can ask a question."

"You may ask," Tsukiyomi said, nodding.

"OK. Why can't you send the spirits to get these treasures back? They take us there anyway. I mean, we're nothing special. Why do you need us to do this? Seems like there's plenty of creatures who can handle this sort of mission in your own…um…dimension."

The god remained silent. His golden eyes studied Kate, who tried not to squirm. She remembered Jinjing standing up to the Greek gods on their last adventure. If wussy Jinjing could face down a god, so could she.

"The spirit guides are not strong enough to defeat a demon," Tsukiyoma said.

"But we are? We're just kids. My Tanuki can turn into a bear. He's loads more powerful than me."

"But he could not wield the dorje."

"Why not?"

Tsukiyomi shook his head. "The dorje is not from our world. It is from your world."

"Yeah, I don't get it. Your Tengu *handed* us the dorje. While we were in *this* world."

The moon god smiled again. "It is hard to understand. I am not the one to give you the answers. But it is your turn now." He bowed low and melted between the trees.

Kate grimaced. "I wish they would stop appearing and disappearing like that. It's downright freaky."

12

Yamachichi

"Now that's one freaky dude," Kate said. She sat astride Tanuki, who had morphed into the fat pony. Behind her, Kitsune—who now sported a new tail, bringing her total up to seven—clip-clopped gracefully and Raahi's bakeneko-horse brought up the rear. They trotted up a beach with black rocks and white sand and approached a very odd man. Wispy white hair covered the old man's entire body. One huge black eye and a tiny blue one poked out of the matted hair. He hobbled on one foot; a thick stick was tied to the stump of his missing leg. He moved towards them, leaning on a cane.

"Got any idea who he is?" Kate said.

Saburo shook his head. "I swear, I'll start studying my mythological spirits as soon as I get back to the real world."

The horses stopped in front of the man and the children slid off their backs.

The old man grinned. Rotting teeth peeked out from behind his hairy lips. "Greetings."

His booming voice shook the ground. Raahi covered his ears. Kate stared at his huge, blinking black eye and the tiny, blue eye which didn't blink at all. She shivered. *Creepy.*

"Who are you?" she asked.

"My name," the old man said, "is Yamachichi."

"Ow," Raahi said. "Stop asking him questions. His voice is loud enough to make us all go deaf."

The old man tried to speak in a whisper which still shook the leaves off a nearby tree. "I have something for you to help you on your journey."

"Another trinket," Kate said. "What do I get?"

The man reached into his cloak. Kate squinted and realized it wasn't a cloak at all, just more thick hair. He hobbled closer. Kate gazed at his hands; she couldn't bear to look into his eyes. The huge one that took up half his face was bad enough, but the little unblinking eye really creeped her out.

A long silver string lay in the man's outstretched hands. Kate blinked. "What am I supposed to do with that? Knit it into a sweater?"

Yamachichi grinned. "This will help you in your next quest."

"Is it a magic string?"

"Magic, yes."

"What does it do?"

The old man shrugged his hairy shoulders. "You will need it to defeat your next demon."

Kate took the soft string and wrapped it around her wrist. She forced her eyes to Yamachichi's face. "What do we do now?"

Yamachichi bowed. "Your spirit guides will take you to where you need to go."

"Of course," Kate said. She turned to her raccoon-horse, but it had disappeared. Instead, a smooth brown dolphin floated in the surf. She shrugged and waded out to meet it.

<<<>>>

RAAHI STARED AT the dolphins. "I'm not going out there," he said.

"You have to," Saburo said.

"But I can't swim. What if I fall off that dolphin? It looks…slippery."

"You haven't come off Bakeneko yet," Saburo said. "Not when he was a horse, or when he was a yak. I doubt you'll fall off now he's a dolphin."

"But I don't like water."

"Then stay here," Saburo said, wading in after Kate.

Raahi stuck out his tongue at the boy's back. He so wanted to throw a handful of sand after Saburo, but while he contemplated it, a hand tapped him from behind. Raahi jumped.

The old man's huge black eye was two inches away from his own. Raahi backed away, into the water. He decided he'd rather brave the sea than deal with this hairy eyeball. He clambered onto

Bakeneko's black and white spotted back and grabbed her dorsal fin.

The dolphins sliced through the water. Every once in a while, they leapt high in the air before plummeting to the sea's surface. Raahi gripped his fin like his life depended upon it, but Kate held her arms high into the air like she was riding a rollercoaster.

"This is awesome! Higher, Tanuki!"

They shot past small green islands rising out of the sparkling sea. Two larger islands loomed ahead. The water became choppy as the current shot between the islands. The dolphins continued their leaps and bounds. Raahi yelped as Bakeneko jumped extra-high and he glimpsed what lay ahead.

Between the two islands, the sea frothed and spun. A huge whirlpool, at least a hundred feet across, swirled in the blue sea.

"I know where we are!" Saburo yelled. "That whirlpool is where the Seto Inland Sea meets the Pacific Ocean."

"It's huge," Kate said.

"And we're heading right for it," Raahi said between clenched teeth.

The dolphins slid towards the whirlpool, riding the current. "I bet we're going into it," Kate said.

"No," Raahi said, his face ashen. "We won't survive."

"We survived jumping into a chasm of boiling sulfur," Kate said. "Chances are, we'll survive this too. Anyway, this has gotta be the portal between this dimension and our dimension. We *have* to go down it."

Raahi shut his eyes. Kate was right, but that didn't help his terror. He hated water. The sight of that spinning maelstrom was too much. He put his head down onto Bakeneko's smooth skin and refused to look up. Kate whooped at the same point his stomach dropped. He dared to open his eyes and stared down into a terrifying blue mass of rolling water. He shut his eyes again. This couldn't possibly end well.

13

The White River

ALISHA SMITH SAT in the small schoolhouse, chewed on her pencil, and gazed out the window. Buried in the jungle, surrounded by banana plants and bamboo, the schoolhouse wasn't much more than a stack of concrete blocks.

The girl turned her attention to the clock, counting down the minutes to when she could put her books away and run into the jungle.

That's where the White River flowed.

They called it The White River because the water was so clear and the white stones lining the bottom shone, reflecting the sun's rays. The river ran down the mountain and spewed into the sparkling Caribbean Sea, miles below.

Alisha loved nothing more than to sit on her favorite rock, splash her sweaty feet in the cold mountain water, and draw. Her family couldn't afford expensive drawing paper, but she drew on every scrap she could find: the margins of old newspapers, the backs of index cards, the jacket of her school notebook. She wore her pencils thin, sketching the lush plants lining the river and the small fish swimming in its currents.

Every once in a while, tourists from the cruise ships anchored down in Ocho Rios would float by, bobbing on inner tubes and drinking warm sodas. They would wave to Alisha and she would flash her white teeth at the foreigners and wave too, wishing she could follow them as they floated down the river, back to their cruise ship and their wonderful, exciting lives.

Alisha's life wasn't exciting at all. Every day she went to school then snuck to the river and drew until the sun set. Then she ran home, late for dinner, only to get a scolding from her mother.

Alisha's mother waited tables in a restaurant and her father carted tourists on sightseeing trips through the jungle. They didn't earn much and sometimes came home late, and they always expected Alisha to have dinner ready when they arrived.

"You don't do much," her mother would say. "You just go to school and draw, and we work late to pay for your things. The least you could do is help make dinner."

Alisha knew she should help her parents more. But she resented the chores. Why couldn't her parents understand how much she loved drawing?

"If you buy me a good sketch pad," she said, "and some nice pencils, I promise I'll have dinner ready every single night."

Her mother rolled her eyes. "We can't afford them things, honey. And if we got them for you, we'd never see you again. You'd camp out near that river and never come home."

Today when the teacher finally told them they could leave, Alisha wandered away from the other kids and pushed her way through the thick foliage to the river bank. Insects buzzed around her and sweat dripped from her brow, but she didn't care. The river water cooled her skin. She dribbled some on her bare arms before she pulled out her paper.

She had extra paper today, Her teacher knew how much Alisha loved drawing and had snuck her a few pieces from the school stockpile. Alisha laid a piece flat on a textbook and chewed her pencil eraser, lost in thought.

What to draw today?

Thick, twisted trees dipped their branches into the crystal-clear river, creating shady spots where fat spiders spun webs and insects buzzed. But she had drawn all those before.

Across the river, the trees rustled and the grasses shook. An animal headed down to the water. Maybe she could draw that. It might be an iguana. Or a mongoose.

Or a crocodile.

Alisha ran a nervous tongue over her lips. Crocodiles were rare around here, but her friend, Benny, had told her he'd seen one twenty feet long just the other day. Of course, Benny tended to exaggerate things.

Her eyes scanned the bank. Two red eyes glared back.

Alisha dropped her precious paper and ran as fast as she could from those evil eyes.

<<<>>>

KATE GRINNED. SHE sat astride Tanuki as he skidded through the aqua water. The hot sun warmed her face. She watched as the island approached; a green jungle dropping into the blue sea.

"Why is it that whenever it's your turn to fight a demon, we end up on a tropical island somewhere?" Saburo said.

Kate wondered if this was Maka's island, the island where her pet parrot Bo lived. Then they passed rickety docks and boats bobbing in the shallow bay, and she knew they were somewhere else. Maka's island only had one living person on it, Maka herself, although Maka wasn't a person but the goddess of the ocean. In Polynesian folklore, anyway.

"We're in present day still," Kate said. "Where do you think we are?"

"Maybe we're in the South Pacific again," Saburo said.

"Look at those palm trees. And all the boats. Ooh…a jerk chicken stand! Man, I'm hungry. Maybe we can stop there for lunch."

"Unless you have money on you, I bet they won't serve us," Saburo said.

But their dolphins weren't stopping at the docks. They swerved around the pier and kept going. Kate laughed as the people lining the docks gawked at them.

"We must look strange, riding on dolphins," Raahi said.

"Pietro was right," Saburo said. "Everyone can see us. If we think our little run-in with the Bhutan demoness made news, this'll make headlines. Look at all the cameras."

A mixture of dark-skinned natives and tourists with wide-brimmed hats and sunglasses crowded the docks, and they all snapped pictures. "Wouldn't that be weird," Kate said, "if we got into the news and our parents saw us?"

Saburo gulped. "Last adventure we had, they never knew we had gone. Do you think this time we're missed?"

Kate hadn't worried about that much, but now she wondered. "Pietro and Jinjing have been talking to us in real time. That means time is moving along like usual. Our parents must be worried sick."

Saburo's frown turned into a smile. "Well, if they see us in the news, at least they'll know we're alive."

"And riding on the backs of dolphins," Kate said, shaking her head. "My dad'll have a heart attack."

The dolphins swam through the bay and headed up a clear river. The hot sun disappeared behind the thick jungle leaves. Water spilled down the mountain, and every once in a while, the dolphins would leap up a waterfall. Kate thought this was great fun until one leap took her right through a sticky spider's web.

"Ugh. I hope there wasn't a spider in it," she said.

"There was a huge one," Raahi said. "Big and hairy."

Kate squirmed. "Is it on me, or is he lying?"

Saburo laughed. "No it isn't on you. But he wasn't lying. That was a scary looking spider."

"I don't like this place," Kate said. "Not if big, hairy spiders are lurking around."

"Uh-oh," Saburo said. "Look up ahead."

A throng of inner tubes, each holding a plump tourist, crammed the thin river from shoreline to shoreline. "How're we gonna get through that unnoticed?" Kate said.

Saburo frowned. "We aren't," he said as the tourists stared at the odd dolphin parade. The dolphins ignored the gasps and camera flashes, and weaved through the tangle of tubes.

"'Scuse me," Kate said. She couldn't help grinning. "Sorry, coming through. Don't spill your soda."

"We're going to be all over the news," Raahi said.

"I can't wait to see the pictures on line," Kate said. "This is so cool. Everybody is going to flip when I get home. I bet I'll be the most popular girl in school after this."

Saburo laughed. "I'm sure you're the most popular girl already."

"What's that?" Raahi asked, pointing towards the far bank. Kate followed his finger with her eyes.

Bright red orbs glared at them between the jungle vines. Kate gulped.

"You think that's our demon?" Saburo said.

Kate nodded. "I'll bet a million bucks it is."

Their dolphins sped past it, up a narrow gorge, and onto a flat, grassy bank. Kate rolled off her dolphin. By the time she hit the ground, the dolphin had disappeared and the raccoon-dog flopped in the grass.

Kate grinned and patted Tanuki's head. "I liked you better as a dolphin, Tanuki. You were less farty."

Tanuki bounded up, followed by Kitsune and Bakeneko. They trotted through the grass and up to a dirt road. The kids scrambled after them.

"It's hot here," Saburo said. "I'm sweating."

"Me too," Kate said. The air was as thick as pudding. Her damp hair stuck to her neck like glue. Saburo rolled up his sleeves. His once white dress shirt was now stained and saggy.

"We need new clothes," he said. "If we're in our time, there's no reason we can't find some."

"Let's worry about that after we get away from those red eyes," Kate said, glancing behind her.

"If that is our demon," Raahi said, "shouldn't we go towards him?"

"We need to follow the guardian spirits," Kate said. "They're heading this way for a purpose."

They followed the trotting animals. The path wound through the thick jungle. Sweat dripped in Kate's eyes.

"Turning into ponies would be really nice right about now," she said to Tanuki.

"There's a house up ahead," Saburo said.

More like a falling-down shack, the corrugated steel structure looked like a good wind would topple it right over. The animals jumped onto the concrete door stoop. Kate knocked on the rusty door.

Two fear-filled black eyes peered through the dirty window. Then the door opened. A girl stood there, her black hair twisted into tight braids and her lower lip trembling. She wasn't any taller than Raahi.

"Who are you?" the girl asked. "Are you lost?"

"No," Kate said, "but we don't know where we are."

A little fear left the girl's eyes, and she smiled. "Then you're lost. You're in the mountains near Ocho Rios."

"Yeah, but where's that? What island is this?"

The girl's eyes got even wider. "You don't even know what country you're in?"

"If we knew we wouldn't be asking."

Saburo elbowed Kate, and she paused. "Sorry, that was rude. I'm Kate, this is Saburo and Raahi. And these are our…uh…pets." She motioned to the animals lounging on the stoop.

The girl took one look at the fox, raccoon-dog, and monstrous cat, and screamed. The rickety house shook as the door slammed shut.

"Poor kid," Kate said. "I forgot Kitsune has seven tails and Bakeneko is super big. And you should stop leering like that, Tanuki. That's enough for even *me* to want to slam the door."

Saburo knocked again. "She must be who we're supposed to meet, or we wouldn't be here."

The door finally opened. "My name is Alisha," the girl said. "An'd you're in Jamaica. And those things aren't real."

"Well, they are, but they're from another dimension," Kate said. "They're our spirit guides."

The girl gulped. "I guess you can come in. Are you spirits too?"

Kate laughed and scooted inside, followed by the boys and the spirit guides. "No, we're just kids. I'm from America, Saburo's from Japan, and Raahi is from India."

"Why are you here?"

"We're here to fight a demon. I know it sounds crazy, but, well, that's what we're here for. Seen any demons around here lately?"

She meant it as a joke, and was surprised when the girl nodded. "The Rollin' Calf. I jus' saw him today."

"The Rollin Calf?" Kate glanced at Saburo. "Does it have red eyes?"

Alisha nodded and her voice fell to a whisper. "That thing is out there somewhere."

"Yeah, we saw it too. Near the river."

Footsteps tromped towards the porch. Everyone froze. Alisha looked petrified.

"It wouldn't come right up to the door would it?" Raahi said.

Alisha gulped. "No, it's even worse. It's my parents. Hide!"

14

The Rollin Calf

THEY HUNKERED IN a small shed and waited. It had been about three hours now. Darkness had fallen. Kate's throat rasped like sandpaper and her stomach growled.

"Where's Alisha? She promised she'd bring us food if we hid in here. And where are those no-good spirit guides of ours?"

"They're probably out getting their dinner," Saburo said, rubbing his stomach. "Wish they'd bring us some."

"The girl, she is probably too afraid to come out here at night," Raahi said. "If she saw the Rollin Calf too, whatever it is, she's probably not going to come here at all."

But the door squeaked and a small figure scooted into the shed.

"I'm sorry," Alisha said. "My parents were talking 'bout you at dinner. They said you swam into the bay on dolphins. Everybody saw it. *Are* you real?"

Kate laughed. "We're human if that's what you mean. But we've been to some unreal places."

"They say you're devils. If they found out you was in the shed, they wouldn't be happy."

She handed Kate some bread and a jug of warm water.

"Thanks," Kate said. She drank big gulps from the jug and bit into the stale bread. She didn't care how it tasted; food was food. "What about you? Do you think we're devils?"

"I think the Rollin Calf is a devil," Alisha said, "and if you're here to stop it, then you must be good."

"What is a Rollin Calf?" Raahi asked.

Alisha's eyes darted about as she whispered. "He's a shape-shifter."

Kate nodded. "Like our animals."

"He mostly takes the shape of a bull, but he can be any animal. The worst though, is if he turns into a black cat."

"What happens then?"

Alisha shook her head. "I dunno, and I don't wanna know."

Kate pulled out her string. "I'm supposed to fight it with this. Do you know how to defeat it?"

Alisha studied the string. "I know if you whip the Rollin Calf with your left hand, you can get rid of it. But you have to watch out for the chains."

"Chains?"

Alisha nodded. "Yeah. They say if you hear the chains rattling, you'll be so paralyzed with fear, you can't move. Then the Rollin Calf will getcha."

Kate chewed her bread and thought. "Anything else?"

"Yeah. The Rollin Calf is afraid of the moon."

"What did she say?" Saburo whispered. "I can't understand her."

Kate gulped the dry bread down. "She says it's afraid of the moon. Hey, we're after the moon god's sword here, aren't we? You think the Rollin Calf took it 'cause he's afraid of the moon god's powers?"

"No," Raahi said. "He didn't take the sword. He's just guarding it."

"How do you figure?"

Raahi gulped some water. "Think about it. The demoness in Bhutan, the Rollin Calf here, do you think they went all the way to Japan to steal from the gods? They aren't gods, they're not powerful enough. They're just spirits, demons. Stuff people way back made up to explain how the world worked."

"But they're real," Kate said. "So they aren't made up at all."

"Someone else stole the treasures," Raahi insisted. "Someone else stole them and left them with demons to guard them until he was ready to take them back."

"And who would that be?"

Raahi shrugged. "I don't know. Another god? Maybe your Japanese gods have enemies. Maybe they're all in some weird god-war, and your Japanese gods are using us to do their dirty work, just like their enemies are using the demons to do theirs. They guard the treasures for their masters, and you're stealing the treasure back for the Japanese gods."

Kate didn't like this idea. "No," she said. "The Japanese gods can't leave their island. Just like the Yellow Dragon couldn't leave his."

"They *say* they can't," Raahi said. "Maybe they just don't want to. Maybe they're too afraid of losing."

Kate hated when he talked like this. "All right, fine. You can say we're here to do some god's dirty work. But it doesn't change the fact that we still have to do it. I've gotta whip this Rollin Calf with my left hand and a silly piece of string so I can defeat it and get the stupid sword back. So, we might as well start. The sooner we get this over with, the sooner we can get home."

"Who's to say we can't leave now?" Raahi said. "We're in the same time, the same dimension. Why can't we ask our spirit guides to take us home?"

"They won't," Kate said.

"Then we turn ourselves in to the nearest embassy and have our parents pay for our return. There's no reason we have to stay here. Not if we're in the real world."

"There is a reason," Kate said. "We need to get the Treasures back."

"Or what? What will happen if we don't?"

Kate couldn't answer. She didn't really know.

<<<>>>

WHEN KATE WOKE the next morning, three pairs of brown eyes stared at her. She blinked.

Alisha sat near her with two curious little boys. "My friends, Benny and Bobby. They wanted to see you."

"It's really them," Bobby, the littlest boy said, touching Kate's hair with his finger. "From the television."

Kate yawned and sat up. "We were on TV?"

Bobby nodded. "Yup. Where are your dolphins?"

"I told you," Alisha whispered. "They aren't really dolphins. They're shapeshifters. They're here to fight the Rollin Calf."

Both Benny and Bobby shuddered. "Why?" Benny said.

"He has a sword we need to take back," Kate said. "Man, am I hungry."

"Here." Alisha unpacked a small box and handed out breakfast. The food tasted greasy and wonderful. Fried plantains, cold fish, more stale bread, all sunk happily into Kate's starved stomach. Better yet, Benny and Bobby brought some worn but clean extra clothes. Saburo exchanged his dress shirt for a t-shirt.

"That feels so much better," he sighed.

"Got any shoes?" Raahi asked.

Benny shook his head. "Sorry, no."

"It was so much easier when Saburo's magic spoon worked," Kate said. "We could just think of what we wanted to eat, and it would appear."

"Really?" Alisha's eyes widened. "That's wonderful magic."

"Yup, but now all we have are the guardians, and they don't do much except take us places. There they are now."

Tanuki snuffled up to the doorway and peered in. Bobby yelped but Alisha, who had met the creatures yesterday, smiled.

"They're not so scary in the daylight. Anyway, we want to help you. It's Saturday, no school. Can we come with you?"

"To find the Rollin Calf? You sure you want to?"

Alisha nodded. "We'll be safe if we're with you."

"You can ride our horses with us," Kate said, yawning.

"What horses?"

Kate nodded towards the guardians. The new kids whipped their heads around. Three ponies stood next to the shed, gazing in.

"Shapeshifters," Bobby whispered.

The ponies took them further up the mountain. They passed ramshackle shacks, huge stands of green bamboo, and an occasional rickety car puttering down the road. The drivers gawked at the ponies and children with wide eyes. One driver ran his car right off the road into a banana tree.

"They know you're the kids from TV," Alisha said. She gripped Kate's waist as the horses trotted even though Kate had explained that it was impossible to slide off Tanuki's back.

"I wonder if my father's seen the news yet," Kate said. "Or if it's big enough news to make it to the States."

"It's big news here," Alisha said. "We'll be famous. But I'm worried about you fighting the Rollin Calf with just a string. Is it magical?"

Kate glanced at the silver string wrapped around her wrist. "I guess it is. A magical creature gave it to me. But I don't know how this soft stuff is going to hurt a demon."

"What do you think you'll have to fight?" Saburo said. "Desire or closed-mindedness?"

"I have no idea. What's that?"

The ponies halted. A yellow dog lay stretched out in the road.

"What a cute doggie," Kate said, smiling. She loved dogs. Except maybe Pug.

Alisha gripped her waist even tighter. "It's the Rollin Calf."

"What, that thing? Where are the red eyes? Where's the chain? It just looks like a dog to me."

"It's a shapeshifta, 'member? The Rollin Calf likes to lie down in roads. So people can't pass through."

"Fine." Kate slipped off Tanuki's back and unrolled the string. "C'mon, poochie. Get outta the road."

The dog raised its head. Its brown eyes changed to red. Lips curled over sharp teeth as a deep growl escaped its throat.

"Oh, dang." Kate backed up. "You're right, Alisha."

The dog rose to face them, teeth bared, ears flat against its head. Kate shuddered at its long claws. The dog shook its head. From around its neck, a little silver bell tinkled.

Kate's heart froze. The fear radiate through her body, from the pit of her stomach down to her legs and up her arms. She couldn't move. Her hand still gripped the string, but she couldn't lift it.

"Kate," Saburo whispered. "Are you OK?"

The others weren't afraid. Didn't they hear the sound? Her whole body trembled.

"Kate," Alisha said. "Get back on the pony."

But Kate couldn't move.

ALISHA GULPED. THERE stood the Rollin Calf in dog-form, growling and shining its red eyes at them, but all fear had left her. She had Tanuki, and Tanuki would protect her from the demon. If Kate were on Tanuki, Kate would be safe too.

She turned to the boys. "She needs to get back on the pony."

Saburo shook his head. "No. It doesn't work that way."

He couldn't explain it in English well, but somehow Alisha understood. Kate had to fight the Rollin Calf on her own. The spirit guardians could step in and help, but they couldn't touch Kate. They couldn't give her any magical powers or she wouldn't be able to wield the string and fight the demon.

"Kate," Saburo said. "It's either desire or closed-mindedness you have to fight, remember that."

But Kate just stood there. Alisha watched, helpless, as the Rollin Calf took a step towards her.

Alisha kicked Tanuki's sides. "Come on, pony. Get in there and help."

The pony jumped, bobbed its head, and leaped between Kate and the Rollin Calf.

AS THE FAT pony blocked her view, Kate's mind cleared. Her first thought was: *Oh no. It's happening again.* The last time she had to fight a demon, she froze. Jinjing had to finish the fight for her. Now here she was, freezing up again. This would not do.

The sound of the bell had done it. The bell around the Rollin Calf's neck. If she could just get close enough to wrest the bell away, she'd have a chance.

But how?

"You're fighting desire, Kate," Raahi said.

Kate gulped. "How do you figure?"

Saburo shot an evil glare at Raahi, then one of Kitsune's flowing tails flicked across his back. His frown faded and he nodded. "He's right, Kate. You're fighting the desire to prove yourself."

"What are you talking about?" Kate hissed.

"You always want to be in charge, you always want everything to go your way. Not because you're selfish, but because you want to prove you can do it on your own. That's your biggest desire."

"So what's the solution then?" Tanuki and Alisha still blocked Kate's view of the Rollin Calf, but the growling intensified. The restless demon pawed at the ground.

"It's changing," Alisha said. "It's shapeshiftin'."

"Ask for help, Kate," Saburo said.

Kate shook her head. "No. I have to do this on my own. This is my task. Nobody else can fight the Rollin Calf but me.

"It's turning into a cat," Alisha whispered.

The slinking black cat shot between Tanuki's legs and leapt at Kate. She raised her hand and let the string fly, but it didn't have any effect. She dodged just in time and the cat landed near her, hissing. It spun around.

"Left hand, Kate!" Alisha said. "You're supposed to use your left hand. Remember the legend."

Kate switched hands. Her left arm felt inept for this. The cat leveled its red eyes on her, flicking its tail. The silver bell around its neck tinkled.

Without Tanuki blocking the cat, the sound's full effect blasted into Kate. Her left arm dropped. Her eyes widened. She couldn't stop her body from shaking.

I can do this, she thought. *I have to do this. On my own.*

Then Tanuki's muzzle brushed her arm. And a rush of understanding engulfed her.

You don't have to do it alone. That's what friends are for. And true friends won't think any less of you if you ask. They want to help you.

"Help me," she whispered.

The cat's eyes narrowed. It got ready to pounce. Before it could, a hand grabbed its collar from behind.

Alisha had reached down from Tanuki's back. She yanked at the Rollin Calf's collar, and it tore in her hand. The little bell fell to the ground and rolled away.

"I've got it, Kate! Go!"

The fearful fog cleared from Kate's mind. The hissing cat retreated a few steps and morphed into a huge black bull with long, sharp horns. It charged.

Kate was ready. She flung her arm forward with all her might and listened to the soft slap as the string whisked across the bull's nose. Then it slammed into her, and she crashed to the ground.

15

The Sword

"I GOT IT all on video. Every bit."

Kate waited for her head to split in two, but it stayed in one piece. She blinked up at Benny, who grinned and waved a camera around.

Saburo's anxious face swam in her blurry vision. "Kate, are you all right?"

"She might have a concussion."

"Who's that?" Kate mumbled. She recognized the voice, but it sounded tinny and far away.

"Jinjing," Saburo said. He held his spoon close to Kate's ear so she could hear.

"I saw you three on TV," Jinjing said. "You were riding dolphins through a bay. Everybody's talking about it."

"Yeah, and they'll be talkin' even more once I post the Rollin Calf fight," Benny said.

"You sure that's a good idea?" Alisha said. "Maybe people shouldn't know about this."

"They're finding out about it anyway," Jinjing said. "They've already figured out you're the same kids who fought the demoness in Bhutan. You're famous."

Kate sat up. She rubbed her throbbing head with one hand.

"Check her pupils," Alisha said. "I got a concussion once, and the doctor checked my pupils. He said if they were really big, I had to be careful. If I fell asleep when my pupils were big, I might not wake up."

"Should we take her to a hospital?" Raahi said.

Kate shook her head. "You kidding? With us being famous? We'd never get away. I'm fine. Just a little dizzy. What happened? 'Cause it didn't feel like I did much with that string."

"It was a magic string, definitely," Saburo said. "As soon as it hit the Rollin Calf, the poor devil shape-shifted into an ant and ran away."

"Did we get the sword?"

"Yes. It was hidden in the bell."

Kate frowned. "The bell?"

Alisha nodded. "The thing around the Rollin Calf's neck that scared you so. When the Calf disappeared, the bell broke open and there was the sword."

"But that bell was the size of a marble."

"It was a magic bell, of course." Alisha held up the sword.

Kate blinked. "That doesn't look like a sword at all. Where's the metal? It looks like it's made out of jade."

"It is," Jinjing's voice said. "It's not a sword you could actually fight with although it's shaped like one. It's a symbolic sword. It's supposed to represent the Japanese Emperor's divinity or something. That's why it's made of jade."

Kate shook her head. "If it's just symbolic, why is everyone fighting for it? What does it matter?"

"It matters to the Japanese gods," Jinjing said. "There must be a reason."

"These treasures are symbolic to us," Raahi said. "Not to them. To them, it is their lifeblood, their soul. If the gods of Japan lose this, they can be defeated."

"I think Raahi is right," Jinjing said. "There's a war going on in the spirit world. Somebody's stealing items of importance to make the other side vulnerable. Like the last time. They stole the Chinese guardians."

"But we got 'em back," Kate said.

"That's right. But now the gods of Japan are under attack."

"By who?" Saburo said.

"It has to be another god," Raahi said. "One who wants power over the others."

Kate frowned. "You still think we're fighting for the wrong side?"

Raahi shrugged. "How are we to know?"

Kate rubbed her head. In the distance she could hear a car puttering up the dirt road.

"We've gotta go," Alisha said. "They're startin' to scout for you. They know you're up here somewhere."

"OK. We're done here, right?" Kate glanced at her

string. She wanted to keep it, but she remembered how Saburo had given Jigme his weapon. And Alisha deserved it. She had helped Kate beat the Rollin Calf.

"Here," she said, handing the girl the silver string. "I don't know if it'll keep its magic, but I'll bet if you ever meet up with the Rollin Calf again, it'll help ya."

The girl smiled. "Thank you, Kate."

Behind them, two men jumped out of the car, cameras snapping away.

"We're gonna sell 'em our video," Benny said. "Well make millions."

Kate grinned. "Maybe not millions, but you'll be famous all right."

"Let's go," Saburo said. Kitsune pranced under him, getting restless.

As the men ran towards them, the horses wheeled and galloped into the jungle. Kate braced herself. She just knew she'd get another spider in the face before this craziness ended.

16

Raahi

THEY PLACED THE sword on the rock and sat, exhausted, in the dewy grass.

"I'm hungry," Kate said.

"The spirit guides will find us some food," Saburo said, stretching out in the grass. "Seems like here they can, but in our world they aren't so good at the food part."

"Are you still there, Jinjing?" Kate asked, twisting her lipstick tube around in her hand.

"I'm still here," Jinjing said.

"So am I," Pietro said. "I'd say 'what did I miss,' but I've just seen it on the internet."

"The whole fight?" Saburo asked.

"The whole thing."

"Great," Kate moaned. "I must've looked like a doofus, just standing there all scared in the pants."

"No, it was pretty amazing. Of course, half the world thinks it's all a big, fake show. But the people who actually saw you do it know it's real."

"What does this all mean?" Saburo said. "The spirits are getting more and more visible in the human dimension."

"Yeah," Kate said. "It's like the dimensions are melding together."

She sat up, stunned by her own comment. "You guys don't think that's what's happening, do you? The two different dimensions, the spirit world and the human world, are starting to fuse together?"

"Could be," Pietro said. "That would explain a lot."

"It sure would," Jinjing said. "I wonder what is going to happen next."

"I'll tell you what I think," Pietro said. "During our first adventure, the human world and spirit world stayed mostly separate. We fought the demons and hardly anybody saw it. Now, people are capturing it on video. And they're starting to believe that something crazy is happening."

"And then what?" Kate said.

"And then...well, this spirit war will start disrupting life in the human dimension. That's what I think."

"And the war won't end until somebody wins," Kate said. "I wish we knew who we were fighting against."

"And if we're fighting for the right side," Raahi put in.

<<<>>>

THAT NIGHT AS he listened to the others snoring in the grass, Raahi lay awake and gazed at the stars. He thought about the last treasure they had to recover: the jewel. What might it be worth if he could get his hands on it? Some wealthy person might pay a huge sum for it, and Raahi would be set for life.

Of course, whoever bought the jewel would lose it eventually. The spirits would come to claim it. But by then, Raahi would have his money and would be living in a tropical paradise somewhere without a care in the world.

Then he thought about what Pietro said. How the human and spirit worlds might be colliding. How it might only be a matter of time before this spirit war disrupted human lives, and not in a nice way. Would he be safe from it all, with his wealth and his island getaway? Or would it matter? Was the Earth doomed if they didn't find a way to stop this war?

Raahi didn't know. And he didn't like these thoughts messing with his perfect plans. Being rich and having many servants—*that* was a good plan, even better than being Ganesh. If the past few days were any indication of what it was like to be a god, he wanted nothing more to do with it. His stomach grumbled, his body ached, and he couldn't get Bakeneko to do anything he wanted her to do. Being a god was definitely not as glorious as he had hoped.

He studied the cat, curled in a ball next to Tanuki. The raccoon dog snored loud enough to wake the dead, but the cat lay with her unblinking green eyes watching him. She didn't trust him. What good was having a spirit guide if it didn't trust you? He knew she'd try to thwart his plans. It was as if she could read all his thoughts.

He glanced at the rock. The sword still lay there, waiting for a god to appear and reclaim it. He itched to take it. But the three spirit guides curled around the rock, and he wouldn't get past them. He sighed and stared at the stars again.

The next task was his. How could he turn it to his advantage?

THE BROTHER AND sister entered the glade, light shining around them and glittering robes flowing behind them. Amaterasu held the sword high and smiled.

"Thank you," she said, bowing. "Only one treasure remains lost."

The kids sat cross-legged in the grass, eating a nice breakfast of rice and fish. Raahi wondered how the spirit guides managed to cook the rice. The food had been waiting for them when they woke, set in black lacquered bowls, silver chopsticks next to each setting. Saburo grabbed the chopsticks and shoveled the food in his mouth. Raahi and Kate had a little more difficulty managing the thin sticks. Kate finally gave up and used her fingers. She was licking them clean when the gods showed up, and she quickly pulled her fingers out of her mouth and wiped them on her jeans.

"It's my turn now, right?" Raahi said.

Amaterasu approached him, smiling. She held out her hands. The boy hesitated before placing his small brown hands in her slender white ones.

The gods hadn't touched the other kids. Only he was singled out for this honor. This must mean he was more important than the others.

But then the goddess focused her deep amber eyes on his, and his elation fell. The idea that she found him unworthy floated through his mind. He was beneath her. He was no god.

"You will have the hardest task," she whispered. "Do you think you're ready?"

Raahi gulped. "I am ready."

But he wasn't. The goddess's eyes searched his. The thoughts he had the night before—stealing the jewel and getting rich—what if she could see? What if she could read his thoughts? What would she do?

But she smiled, dropped his hands, and moved her gaze to the spirit guides. Tanuki rolled and yawned in the grass, Bakeneko purred and rubbed her back against the rock, and Kitsune swished her now eight tails in the air. She only had one more tail to go before she reached the magical number of nine.

"Where are we going next?" Kate asked.

Amaterasu smiled. "Your guides will show you. We will see you soon." She faded into the woods, followed by her silent brother.

"Of course," Kate said. "You can never get a straight answer from any of these gods. Why don't they just tell us?"

"Maybe they don't know," Saburo said.

"Of course they know. The spirit guides take us to the right place every time. If they know, you can bet the gods controlling them know. Oh well. At least we got some breakfast in us."

"And looks like out transportation is ready," Saburo said.

Raahi frowned at their new mode of conveyance. "Goats? Why goats?"

"That's gonna be uncomfortable," Kate said. "Those goats are awfully bony. How do we sit on 'em?"

"You can hold onto the horns," Saburo said, mounting his Kitsune-goat. "They aren't so bad."

AMATERASU'S GAZE TROUBLED Raahi. He didn't like the guilty feeling her eyes gave him. Like he shouldn't be thinking the bad things he had thought.

But why not? What was wrong with making a little money off this venture? He wasn't hurting anybody, except somebody gullible enough to buy the jewel. Anyone who could afford it could stand to lose some money anyway. Help the less fortunate. Share the wealth. And the gods would still get their precious jewel back, unharmed.

Underneath him, Bakeneko bucked. The boy was in no danger of falling off, but the kick jarred him from his devious thoughts.

"Did you do that on purpose?" he hissed.

"Look," Saburo said. "We're nearing Mt. Fuji."

"Wow," Kate said. "That's the mountain you see in pictures of Japan. Do you live near here, Saburo?"

"No," Saburo said. "In fact, the only time I've been near Mt. Fuji was when we were passing it on the trip to my father's funeral. I couldn't see it then. It was blocked by the clouds."

Now the huge mountain loomed ahead, perfectly cone-shaped and covered with snow, stark white against the blue sky. No towns crowded the hillsides around it, no trains flew by. In this place—in the spirit world—the mountain rose out of a serene forest. Only the twittering birds broke the silence.

The goats entered the forest. Saburo gazed at the tall, twisty trees. "Do you two know where we are?" he asked.

"We're in Japan," Kate said.

Saburo gripped Kitsune's goat horns. "I know that. I mean this forest. I think we're in Aokigohara."

"Aokigo-what?"

"Aokigohara. The Sea of Trees."

"Doesn't sound too bad," Kate says.

"It's also known as the Haunted Forest of Death."

Kate sighed. "Not so good. What's supposed to live in it? The bogeyman? Vampires? What?"

"No, nothing like that. Well, there's legends of course. But people come here…to die."

"What, on purpose?"

Saburo nodded. "People die in here all the time. They wander in and can't find their way out. Some don't mean to get lost, but others do it on purpose if they're really depressed."

Kate gulped. "Creepy."

"Yes, but we have the spirit guides," Saburo said. "So we should be OK."

Raahi listened to Saburo's broken English and began to tremble. He didn't understand why, but Saburo's story about getting lost and not finding your way out scared him more than anything else that had happened on this journey. He did not like these woods. The dark trees grew in twisted clumps, blotting out the sun. They couldn't even use the sun as a compass if they got lost in here. And everywhere he looked he saw sinkholes and dark rocky crevices. He shuddered. He hated deep, dark holes.

"Let's get out of here," he said, trying to turn Bakeneko around. She paid no attention and kept plodding between the trees.

Raahi panicked. He tried to jump off the animal's back, but couldn't. He pounded his fist on Bakeneko's neck and screamed, but she ignored him. Frustrated tears spilled down his cheeks.

"Get a grip, Raahi," Kate said. "You're perfectly safe with your spirit guide. Just relax."

Raahi took some deep breaths. He stared with bloodshot eyes at the others. They were calm, even Saburo who knew all about this awful place. Kate looked at him with pity in her eyes. Saburo shot him a scornful look. He wiped his nose on his sleeve and anger replaced his fear. He berated himself for showing any weakness to these two. How would he ever gain their fear and respect if they thought he was a big baby?

"I wonder why the gods sent us here," Saburo said.

Kate shrugged. "Well, at the start of all this, Tengu gave you the dorje, and Yamachichi gave me the magic string. I'd guess there's a spirit in these woods that has to give Raahi a trinket to defeat the next demon."

Raahi fought down his panic. "We'd better find him soon," he said.

Kate nodded. "Yeah. Just thinking about meeting up with dead people in these woods is getting me a little freaky."

"Yes, but we're in the spirit world. There are no dead people here." Saburo scratched Kitsune between her horns and added, "I hope."

17

Oni

AFTER RIDING FOR almost more than he could bear, they came to a clearing. Raahi still couldn't see the sun. He wondered if the branches coiled and twisted together on purpose to block out the light and make sure their victims couldn't escape. He was so busy staring at the tangled branches, he barely heard Saburo's sharp intake of breath.

Raahi looked ahead and yelped. If he could have gotten off Bakeneko, he would have tumbled backwards and run into the forest, scary trees or not.

In the middle of the rocky clearing, staring at them with stony eyes, sat a huge creature. Its red skin glinted in the meager sunlight. Two sharp horns jutted from the beast's head. It looked almost human with its huge muscles, burly chest, and feet like boulders. A swath of tiger skins was wrapped around its waist.

"Hey," Kate whispered. "I know what that is. That's the demon you're always going on about, isn't it, Saburo?"

"It's an oni." Saburo whispered. His eyes glowed and he *smiled* at that ugly, brutish monster.

Raahi didn't like the looks of the demon one bit. The oni turned his red eyes on Raahi and gave him a creepy glare. Raahi was pretty sure the monster didn't care for him any more than he cared for it.

Bakeneko bucked again, and this time Raahi did fly off, landing right next to the monster's huge wooden club. He scrambled to his feet and backed away, waiting for the club to smash his head.

The oni grunted and pointed a massive finger at the boy.

"He wants you," Saburo said.

"Wants me for what?" Raahi scooted backward and bumped into Bakeneko, who poked him with her horns.

"He's probably got your trinket," Kate said. "You'd better go get it."

Raahi didn't want to get anywhere near the oni, but the sharp pokes from his goat-cat forced him forward. His heart hammering, he finally stood and forced his eyes to the demon's. He didn't see any kindness in those eyes, only an annoyed resignation. The oni didn't want to help him but didn't have much choice.

"*You* seem pleased to see it," he said to Saburo. "Why don't you find out what it wants?"

"No, this is your task," Saburo said, sounding envious. "I wish I could approach it, but Kitsune won't let me off her back. I've always wanted to meet an oni."

"Why?" Raahi kept his eyes on the oni's club as he inched forward. "It doesn't look pleasant."

"Oh, it depends with an oni. He can be helpful, or devious. Just like any spirit. But I'm sure this oni is here to help us. Otherwise, the spirit-guides wouldn't have brought us to him."

Raahi knew this was probably true, but he still didn't trust the oni. He flinched as its fist plummeted towards his head. The fist just missed, instead opening in front of Raahi's nose.

A small silver object lay on the oni's outstretched palm. The oni grunted.

"Pick it up," Kate said.

Raahi gulped. He didn't want to touch the oni's red skin. It might burn like fire. His shaky fingers reached out and gripped the silver object. The oni grunted again and moved its fist away.

"What is it?" Kate said.

Raahi pulled his wary eyes away from the demon. "It's a box."

He opened it. Red velvet covered the insides, but the box was empty.

"How're we supposed to fight a demon with a box?" Kate said.

Raahi shrugged and stuffed the box into his pocket. He turned away from the oni and climbed on Bakeneko's back. "We've got what we came for. Let's get out of this wood."

"You should say thank you to the oni," Saburo said.

"Why don't you do it?" Raahi said. "You're so in love with onis, he'd probably take it better from you."

<<<>>>

KITSUNE TRIPPED CLOSER to the demon and Saburo found he could slide off her back. Now that he was actually standing before his hero demon, his legs shook a little beneath him. He gulped, trying to get some moisture in his throat, and bowed.

"*Domo arigato gozaimasu*," he said. "Thank you, Oni."

The oni's hard eyes softened. It turned to Saburo and bowed too, smiling. That smile might scare the pants off most people, but Saburo thought his heart would burst with happiness. All fear left him and he smiled back.

The oni brought one finger close to the boy. Saburo wrapped his hand around it. A comforting warmth spread from the smooth finger into Saburo's hand and coursed through his body. Strength flooded through him as if he had drunk a magic elixir that would give him the power of a thousand men.

He let go of the oni's finger and skipped back to Kitsune.

"Saburo," Kate whispered. "Your limp."

"What about it?" he asked, still smiling.

"Don't you feel it? It's not there anymore. It's gone."

<<<>>>

THEY RODE THROUGH the woods in silence. Always moving forward, but quickly now, as if the spirit-guides knew their mission here was done and wanted to get out as fast as they could. But as far as Kate could tell, they were moving farther in.

When they finally broke free of the woods, Mt. Fuji loomed ahead. They made a beeline for it.

"Now that Raahi has the trinket," Kate said, "I guess the spirit guides will be taking us out of the Spirit Japan, back to the real world. We went through a pool of sulfur and a whirlpool the last two times. How do you think we'll leave here this time?"

Saburo didn't answer. He swung his legs and gazed down at them, like he still couldn't believe it.

"How do they feel?" Kate asked.

"Not stiff. For the first time since the accident the hip feels great. Anyway, maybe we'll leave here through Fuji-san.

"How? A cave?"

"Maybe through the volcano part."

Kate gulped. "Mt. Fuji is a volcano?"

"Of course it is. You can't tell from the cone shape? And see the little wisp of smoke up there? In the human world, it hasn't erupted for ages, but it's still an active volcano. Maybe we have to jump into it."

"I don't like that idea. You remember the last time I had to enter a volcano? That didn't work out so well."

"It worked out great. We defeated Pele and released the Vermillion Bird from captivity."

"You mean *Jinjing* defeated Pele and released the bird. I didn't help. I just stood there like a big idiot. I don't like volcanos, Saburo. They haven't been kind to me."

Saburo grinned. "I don't think volcanos are kind. Or evil. They're just mountains filled with hot rocks. Anyway, I bet once we jump in, we'll end up back in our world in an instant. That's what's happened the other times."

They made their way up the mountain in silence. The goats skittered up the faint paths, first winding between trees, then shuffling through black, crumbly rock. The mountain climbed into the clouds; they couldn't see the top. The goats clattered into the fog. Kate shivered.

In the mist, a hand grabbed hers. She yelped, thinking the hand might belong to a ghost, but it felt warm. Saburo's hand. She gripped it, feeling better.

If Saburo stood beside her, she wouldn't hesitate to jump into Fuji's fiery depths.

18

Aali

Raahi wished he had a turban, like his uncle wore. If he had a turban, he could put it on his head and shade his face from the relentless sun. His throat felt drier than the desert they had been wading through for the past few hours.

"Oh, why didn't I bring a hat?" Kate moaned behind him.

Raahi didn't care if Kate was miserable. He didn't care that he finally rode out in front, leading the group, he didn't even care about the jewel anymore. All he cared about was water. Sweet, sweet water.

But all he saw was sand. Sand that stretched out to meet the horizon. Brown sand mixed with brown rocks, as far as he could see. Not a drop of water in sight.

He didn't like how high up he rode, either. He hadn't realized camels were so tall. Below him, Bakeneko swayed back and forth on her camel legs. Raahi sat cross-legged on her hump. He couldn't fall off. But looking at the ground still made him dizzy.

He licked his dry lips. "Why do we have to go through this desert? Why can't the spirit guides appear at the place we're supposed to be, instead of making all these long, pointless journeys?"

"Maybe they get to our world through wormholes," Kate said. "Maybe the wormhole can only spit them out in certain places. Maybe they can't go exactly to where they need to go."

"You'd think if they were gods, they could pop up any place they like."

"They aren't gods. They're spirits. The gods can't leave Japan, remember?"

Raahi shook his head. How could he respect these "gods"? Gods so weak they couldn't leave their own territories. What good were they? He fingered the silver box in his pocket. He wondered how much money he could get for it.

"So, why were you so scared in the forest?" Kate said.

Raahi blinked. "Why are you asking?"

"I'm just curious. You've been so…standoffish about everything else. Nothing seems to faze you, except for the screaming demoness in Bhutan, but you totally flipped out in the woods. Why?"

"I don't want to talk about it," Raahi said.

"Fine, don't. Just remember, the poisonous delusion you're going to have to deal with is closed-mindedness.

Maybe you can start by not being so closed-*mouthed* about things."

"I'm not closed-minded," Raahi said.

"You must be," Kate said, "or you wouldn't have this task."

"Stop talking to me," Raahi said. Behind him, Kate fell silent. Raahi seethed on his camel. He knew why the forest scared him so. But he sure didn't want to let Kate or Saburo know.

WHEN RAAHI WAS so young he could barely remember, he fell down a well. Not a deep well—it was just getting excavated—but deep enough so he couldn't get out.

He had been playing in the dirt lot behind his house when the two boys showed up. Raahi was drawing in the dirt with a stick. A shadow fell over him. The air grew still. He looked up.

Aadi's sneering face, and his sniveling lackey Prajeet's, hovered over him. He gulped and dropped his stick.

"Raahi," Aadi said, "quit playing in the dirt like a monkey." He kicked dirt into Raahi's face.

"Like a monkey," the parrot Prajeet repeated. He grinned an evil grin and pushed Raahi so the smaller boy's face smacked into the dirt.

Raahi's heart clenched, first with fear, but then with another emotion: anger. He licked the dirt off his lips and crunched it between his teeth. He jumped to his feet, eyes blazing.

"You'll get what's coming to you, Aadi Patel," he said.

Aadi's eyes narrowed. His lips curled over crooked teeth, and Raahi's fear came back in a rush. He took off running.

The boys gave chase, but Raahi knew every back alley, every dead end, and every hidden detour. He lost his pursuers after running hard for a solid five minutes. He glanced behind him. The boys had gone.

He didn't notice the hole until he slid into it, landing with a thud at the bottom.

Although the sides were soft, he could not get a grip and pull himself out. Raahi had run right off the street and into a vacant lot where they were digging a well. He screamed and cried and begged, but the workers had gone home and nobody else wandered close enough to hear his screams.

Darkness fell.

Exhausted, hungry, thirsty, and all cried out, Raahi sank to the damp ground. He listened to the soft rain beginning to fall. The rain turned into a torrent. Raahi huddled in the hole, praying the sides wouldn't cave in or he wouldn't drown in the water.

In the darkness, every sound, every bolt of lightning, every dog's howl, drilled the fear deeper into his heart. But after a while, he could fear no more. The hatred set in. Hatred for the boys who had done this to him. Raahi swore he'd get revenge.

They pulled him up the next morning when the workmen came to finish digging. As soon as his mother stopped making a fuss over him, Raahi started planning. He couldn't beat Aadi and Prajeet with brawn. He'd have to beat them with cunning.

That day Raahi, who had been bullied himself, became the biggest bully of all. His fear of both water and confined spaces began that day, also. He didn't like thick woods either. But he learned to hide his fears in front of others. He hated himself for showing his weakness to Saburo and Kate.

"WHAT'S THAT UP ahead?" Kate asked.

Raahi could barely open his salty, crusty eyes. His could hardly move his parched tongue over his dry lips. He peered between Bakeneko's ears. A green smudge broke the plane between sand and sky.

"Trees. I think I see trees."

The camels broke into a quick jog. They weren't thirsty or tired like the humans they carried, but they knew their charges needed sustenance to survive this horrible desert.

"I hope it's not a mirage," Kate said.

It wasn't. Water from some unknown source bubbled up in this arid place. Tall palms and bushy plants grew around the deep water hole, sucking up the life-giving liquid. Near the hole, a white horse grazed on green grass and a boy lay yawning in the hot sun.

Raahi ignored the horse, the boy, and his fear of deep water. He slipped off Bakeneko's hump and flung his face into the pond, slurping the cool liquid in long gulps. He had never tasted anything so amazing.

<<<>>>

Aali

KATE WONDERED ABOUT the oasis's other occupants. The horse's white coat sparkled in the sunlight. The boy's robe was even whiter. She could hardly focus on either of them.

"Do you think they're real," Saburo whispered, "or are they spirits?"

"I dunno. They look awfully content. Like they live here. 'Scuse me!" she called.

The boy raised his turban-covered head. He gazed at her with dark eyes, but didn't speak.

"Yeah, definitely a spirit of some kind," she said. "Hey Tanuki, let me down, willya?"

Tanuki grunted and lay down. Kate hopped off and gave Tanuki's camel head a pat before jumping to the side as he spat, quite a long distance, and burped.

"You're even disgusting as a camel," she said. "You really are hopeless, Tanuki."

If the boy really were a boy, he'd be about sixteen or so. But Kate had the gut feeling this boy was much older. He might be a thousand years old, for all she knew. "Are you real," she asked, "or a spirit?"

The boy frowned. "I don't understand. My name is Aali. I am a genii."

"Like the kind that can grant wishes?" Raahi said.

The boy looked puzzled. "Guess not," Kate said. "*Can* genii grant wishes?"

Aali shook his head. "We have great magic. But we do not normally grant wishes to humans."

"Another myth gone wrong," Kate said. "What do you do, then, as a genii?"

"I am here to fight the ifrit."

"The what?"

"The ifrit. The evil genii."

"We're here to fight something too," Kate said, "although we don't know what. We're trying to get our jewel back. Well, the Japanese gods' jewel. Can you help us?"

The genii studied her. "I believe we may be fighting the same thing. I had a dream that I must wait here and my help against the ifrit would come."

"Well, here we are," Kate said. "But we need a rest first. And food would be great if you have any."

"There are some fig trees over there," Aali said, "but I can find better food for you if you like."

"Cool beans," Kate said before finally succumbing and joining Raahi and Saburo at the water hole. She drank as much as her stomach could hold, then she threw water on her face. The air felt cooler in this shady place, but washing the sweat off her face still helped.

"What did he say?" Saburo asked.

"He's a djinn," Raahi said.

"A genii," Kate corrected.

"It's the same thing," Raahi said.

"I have food for you," the genii called.

Kate turned around. Her stomach grumbled in excitement. The most incredible feast she had ever seen lay spread out on the grass.

19

The Ifrit

"Now this is more like it," Kate said, staring at the mounds of food. "Just like old times, right Saburo? Like when your wooden spoon could make any food we wanted."

Saburo nodded. He and Kate sat and dug in. Raahi stood, undecided. He wasn't sure if he should touch the food or not. It was enchanted food, and that couldn't end well. Then his stomach rumbled, and he gave in and sat next to Saburo.

Kate grabbed a huge leg of lamb. Next to her, Saburo dug into a bowl of steaming rice. Raahi picked at some almonds. He tasted one. It crunched between his teeth like an almond ought to, and he decided then and there that it may be enchanted food, but it was still food. He stuffed a whole slice of flatbread into his mouth and grabbed a slab of cheese.

"There is plenty," Aali said, watching him with amusement. "We do not have much time, but slow down, please. Enjoy."

"Why don't we have much time?" Kate asked.

The boy genii frowned. "The ifrit are on the move."

Raahi gulped his bread down. He wasn't sure what an ifrit was, but he didn't like the sound of it.

"The bad genii?" Kate said.

Aali nodded. "There are all types of genii. Some are good, some are bad. Some are a little bit of both. I am a good genii. I keep balance in the world. But the ifrit are pure evil."

"And they have our jewel?"

"I am not sure, but only an ifrit could steal from a god. And if the jewel belonged to the gods, well, the ifrit could wreak some havoc with it if it's in their possession."

"Do you know why they'd want to do that?" Kate asked.

The genii frowned again. "They want to start a war."

Inside, Raahi smiled. He had been right. Now he had to decide what to do. Should he recapture the jewel and return it to the Japanese gods? Or should he side with the ifrit?

His thoughts drifted to his father, who loved old fairy stories. His especial favorites were the 1001 Arabian Nights. In those tales, genii granted wishes, made incredible things happen, and made their owners rich.

Maybe the ifrit could make him even more rich and powerful than the jewel could.

But what could he barter with? They already had the jewel. How could Raahi convince the ifrit that he was on their side? That he could provide a valuable service to them? That they should reward him with wealth and power?

He glanced up. The young genii studied his face. Just like Amaterasu's gaze, the genii's eyes probed into Raahi's mind, deciphering his plans. He forced himself to switch his train of thought.

"You say the ifrit are on the move," he said to Aali. "Why? Where are they going?"

"They are headed to the city," Aali said, nodding towards the horizon. "Ifrit work best in places where they have plenty of human thoughts and feelings to feed off of. They will have great power there. But the good genii are gathering forces to meet them."

"And what will happen then?"

"We will have a great battle. A fight. If we succeed, we can banish the ifrit. If we fail, they will take over the world."

"Well, we can't have that," said Kate.

"Do they have a leader?" Raahi said. "I don't want to fight all of them. Kate, you only had to fight one spirit. So did Saburo. I can't be expected to fight a whole army of evil genii."

"The ifrit fall under the greatest, the most evil genii ever," Aali said. "His name is Shaitan."

Raahi gulped. He didn't know why, but the name caused his insides to go icy numb. Even though he had drunk his fill of the cool, clear water in the oasis, his mouth went drier than the dusty desert surrounding them. His hand reached into his pocket and he gripped the silver box. He wondered if he could handle this.

"As far back as when time began," Aali said, "the good djinn of the world have fought off the ifrit's evil powers. Before, the ifrit had always worked alone. They didn't like sharing power, even with each other. It was easier to keep them in check. But now, Shaitan has bonded them together. And together, they are incredibly powerful. Even with our good djinn, we are afraid we might lose this battle.

"But the other night I had a vision. Through a sand-storm rode three strangers. I could not see their faces. I did not know who they were. But I knew if I waited here, they would find me. They would help us win."

He gazed at the three kids and their camels lying in the grass. "I don't know where you came from," he said, "but you must be who I'm waiting for."

"Can I ask a question?" Kate said. "Are we in the human world here, or the spirit world?"

The djinn shook his head. "I do not know. The djinn reside in a world where humans cannot tread. Some-times we are called to their world, but it has been centuries now since we have visited that place."

Kate gazed at the blue sky marred only by a streak of white. "That looks like an airplane exhaust to me," she said. "Saburo?"

Saburo looked up from his meal and nodded. "Yes. We must be in the human world."

Aali grimaced. "If you are right, it would be the first time in many centuries I have broken the plane and entered the human realm. How could I not know this had happened?"

"I dunno," Kate said, "but lots of weird things have been happening lately. The two worlds are mixing."

The djinn frowned. "This is not good. This is wrong."

"Tell me about it," Kate said. "And if you're going to fight a war against these evil genii, you can bet you're gonna be on display for all the humans to watch."

"Can you imagine if the cameras capture this?" Raahi said. "A genii war?"

"It'll cause chaos and mayhem all over the place," Kate said.

"Just what the demons would want," Saburo said.

Aali adjusted his turban. "I wonder if they realize it. That they're entering the human world. I didn't realize it. The other good djinn may not realize it either. Something bigger is happening, I think."

Kate nodded. "That's what we think too. And for some reason, we're caught in the middle of it."

"This city," Raahi said. "The city you say the evil djinn are heading for. Where is it? Is it a spirit city?"

Aali shook his head. "It is a special city. A city where the genii can move from our world to the human world. The city exists in both places. But the ifrit will head to the human world. They must feed on humans to gain strength."

Raahi gulped. "Feed?"

Aali locked eyes with the boy and nodded. "Ifrit feed on human souls. They will gain great power if we do not reach the city before they do."

"What happens to the people if the ifrit get there first?" Kate asked.

"They become shells, wasted. They are still living, but they are not whole."

"Like zombies?"

Raahi shuddered. "Don't say zombies, please."

"Where's your army now?" Saburo said.

"I have called the djinn. I have warned them of the importance. They will come."

Raahi scrutinized the boy genii. He might be an ancient being, but he looked young. He also didn't seem that experienced. "How many good djinn are there?" he asked.

Aali frowned. "What do you mean?"

"I mean, when you call this army of yours, how many genii will show up?"

Aali shook his head. "I do not know. Each djinn rules a certain region. My area lies in this desert. I have never strayed from it. I have gone as far as the city's outskirts, but have never entered it."

"So basically, you have no idea if anybody will actually show up to help fight these bad djinn?"

"They will come."

"But how many?"

Aali could not say. Raahi decided right then that he was fighting for the wrong side. This side was sure to lose. The side of the ifrit was the powerful side. The winning side. The side he wanted to be part of.

20

The Lost City

"You should show Aali the box," Kate said.

Raahi's fingers gripped the object in his pocket. "Why?"

"He might know what it is. The oni gave it to you to fight whatever it is we need to battle next. I'll bet it's that Shaitan guy. He's got the jewel. So, you'll have to battle him with that box. Aali might know what it's for."

Raahi didn't want to ask Aali about the box. The box was a bargaining chip. If this Shaitan fellow feared it, Raahi could use it for a swap—the box for the jewel. He didn't need to know what the box did to use it that way. And he didn't need any help from Aali.

"I bet Jinjing could tell you what it is just by looking it up on her computer," he said.

Kate gazed at the lipstick tube clutched in her hand. "Yeah, but she isn't answering. Neither is Pietro. I wish they'd pick up their magical objects. I'd like to warn them about what's coming. Let 'em know where we are."

"We don't *know* where we are," Saburo said. He jogged around the small oasis, a goofy grin on his face. Raahi frowned at him. Maybe Saburo couldn't have run like that before, but that wasn't any excuse for him to show off now. Raahi had never liked Saburo, but now he didn't trust him either. The oni had healed that boy, and in an unnatural way. Sooner or later, it would come back to bite Saburo in the butt. The oni would want his payment for such a great gift.

The idea that maybe Saburo had already earned the oni's gift was lost on him; he couldn't fathom such a notion.

Raahi was also glad that Pietro's and Jinjing's disembodied voices hadn't popped up on this leg of the journey. Those kids always sounded superior, like they were telling everyone what to do. Raahi didn't like anyone telling him what to do, especially two kids who weren't even part of this adventure, kids just calling out plays from the sidelines.

Saburo finally stopped showing off, as if running was anything special, and flopped on the grass next to Kate, breathing hard.

"So where do you think we are?" Kate asked. "I mean, Aali says we're in a desert near a city, but that could be hundreds of places. There's a desert around Cairo in Egypt, and the Gobi desert in Asia probably has some cities too."

"No, we must be in Arabia," Raahi said. "That's why we've met up with a genii. Geniis live in Arabia, right? Like Iran and Iraq, and all those places."

Kate frowned. "I've asked Aali, but he doesn't know. He just knows there's a city near here."

Raahi snorted. "He doesn't know much of anything if you ask me."

"He's sure scant on information," Kate said, which surprised Raahi. Normally she disagreed with him, mostly, he thought, to annoy him.

They glanced over to where the genii stood, saddling his horse. "You'd think if he were truly magical that horse would saddle itself," Raahi said.

"Or he wouldn't need a saddle at all," Kate said. "Like us with our spirit guides. We just stick to their backs."

"It is time," Aali called. "We must head towards the city."

"Oh goody," Kate said, standing. Raahi agreed. He had no desire to traipse across that desert again, but sitting around in this oasis bored him. He headed towards the genii, who studied him before turning his gaze to the other two.

"You all must have more suitable clothing," he said. "The desert is no place for the clothes you have now."

He blinked, and Raahi looked down. A cool linen garment floated around him, just like the Arabs wore in old movies. A turban covered his hair and face to keep the dust and sun away. He turned towards the others, who were decked out in the same garb.

"Now we fit in," Kate said.

Raahi couldn't help smiling. Kate annoyed him most of the time, but even though the new clothing covered every inch of her, he was pretty sure Kate would stand out no matter where they went. She was too graceful, too beautiful not to.

They clambered aboard their camels and trotted away from the oasis. As soon as they left it the sun slammed into them, but the new clothes let the breeze in and the headdresses kept the sun off their faces.

"What's gonna happen when we reach the city?" Kate called to Aali.

The genii turned his horse. "There, the djinn will gather. And we will confront the ifrit."

"Already?"

Kate didn't sound happy about meeting evil genii so soon. But Raahi was glad to hear it. The sooner he could convince the ifrit of his loyalty, the sooner he'd be away from these horrible kids and that self-righteous djinn. He gripped the silver box in his pocket. He didn't want to lose it. If it could help defeat an ifrit, they'd give him anything for it, he was sure of that.

THE CLIFFS BLENDED with the desert; that same sandy color covered everything. Raahi watched, fascinated, as they approached a chasm between two tall cliffs. They plowed through the sand and entered the chasm, the sunlight disappearing behind the towering cliffs. Shadows enveloped them. They trotted forward, the camels' feet shuffling through the sand. Raahi squinted, trying to glimpse what lay ahead.

Kate, who had somehow gotten ahead of Raahi, yelped. "Saburo! Do you know where we are?" I've seen this in movies."

They burst into a wide, open area, the solid blue sky hanging overhead. In front of them, carved into the sandstone cliff, stood a columned façade, like an entrance to an old Grecian temple. Six rock columns rose into the air, meeting up with a beautiful carved pediment. Smaller columns rose above the pediment, carved right into the rock.

"We're in Petra," Kate said.

Raahi stared around in amazement. The lost city of Petra. He had watched a TV special on it once and had held a fascination with the place ever since. His whole body tingled with excitement. Petra, an ancient city completely carved into the cliffs, and here he stood, right in the main square.

"But nobody lives here," Kate said. "Why would the ifrit come to a place where nobody lives?"

Aali looked puzzled. "The last time I visited, this city was full of people."

"That must've been thousands of years ago," Raahi said. "If the ifrit come here looking for humans to feed on, they're going to be disappointed."

He looked around. A few tourists snapped photographs. A fat man with a big cowboy hat sat on a miserable-looking camel and stared at them. Raahi guessed that camels and horses were common here, but not a red camel with eight stubby tails, or a swirly black and white one, or a stallion so white it glowed in the sunshine.

"Hey!" the cowboy yelled. "Ain't you the kids from TV?"

His camel shuffled towards them. The cowboy hat tottered on the fat man's head. Raahi sat silent as he approached, mesmerized by the man's huge gut, which jiggled as the camel moved.

"You're the ones who rode the dolphins in Jamaica, ain't you? And fought that weird shape-shiftin' monster. I saw it on the internet." He pulled the camel to a halt in front of Aali's horse and snapped some pictures. Then he gazed at the genii. "Who're you?"

"I am Aali," the genii said, "and you are in the way."

"The way to what?" Fear filled the man's eyes. "There ain't another demon around here, is there?"

"There will be," Raahi said, "if you wait long enough."

"Yeah, you might want to tell everyone here to clear out," Kate said. "We're expecting a mass of ifrit any minute."

The man gulped. He might not know what an ifrit was, but it sounded ominous enough. He snapped one last picture before yanking his camel around and joining the less brave souls who had their cameras aimed at the strange group from a distance.

"They'd better all clear out," Raahi said, "if they don't want to become food for the ifrit."

Kate nodded. "Yeah, we don't need a band of zombies on top of everything else. You sure they're gonna come here, Aali?"

"This is the city where the ifrit always meet," Aali said. "But my people, the good djinn, they will meet here too. We will repel the ifrit from this world."

"Where are they, then?" Kate asked, gazing around. "Nobody's here but us."

Saburo stilled, his ears straining. "I hear something. It's coming from behind us. Sounds like hoof beats."

They turned their camels around and watched as several large horses paraded through the gorge and into the city. Some genii wore flowing white garb like Aali, but some were decked out in bright colors while others wore heavy mail made of gold or silver that glinted in the sunlight.

Someone yelled, "Holy cow!" Raahi turned his head. The large man with the cowboy hat had dropped his camera into the sand. His mouth hung open and his eyes bulged. The other tourists ran for it, hoping to get away from the ever-increasing mass of genii.

"These are the good guys, right?" Kate whispered to Aali.

"Yes. These are the genii I called."

"There aren't many of them," Saburo said.

In the end, about fifty genii gathered in the city center and Aali trotted away from the camels to meet them.

Kate turned to Raahi. "The fight's coming soon and we still don't know what your box does. You need to ask the genii. I'll bet they know."

"That box looks a lot like the one Jinjing had, remember?" Saburo said. "Except this one is silver. You think something comes out of it when you open it?"

Kate shrugged, then her face brightened. "Or something goes in it."

"What do you mean?" Raahi said.

"Well, you've heard stories of genii, right? How they live in bottles? Maybe this is the bottle to trap the ifrit."

"But it isn't a bottle. It's a box."

"So? Remember what Pietro said: how humans developed these myths, but none of 'em were spot-on? I'll bet you my tanuki that your box will capture Shaitan."

Raahi ran one finger over the box, wondering if Kate was right. If so, he could capture the most evil genii alive. And how did the myth go? Once you had a genii in a jar, it had to grant you wishes? But Aali had said that wish-granting didn't really happen. Was he right, or was he lying?

Raahi thanked his stars he hadn't asked the genii about the box. If Aali knew what he held, the genii would steal it for himself. Especially if what Kate said was true and Raahi held the way to imprison a genii. Maybe it could work on any genii, not just Shaitan. Maybe if Raahi traded Shaitan the jewel for this box, the ifrit could use it to capture and defeat the "good" genii.

Thought after thought tumbled over in his devious mind. He was so busy thinking out a plan, he didn't notice the hush that fell over the city.

A DARK CLOUD rolled across the sky, casting its shadow over the grouped riders. A low rumble filled the air. Saburo gulped. "What's happening now?"

"It must be the ifrit," Kate said, as a cold wind whipped her linen headdress away. She clutched Tanuki's neck, hunkered down, and tried to keep her eyes focused on the black cloud. "I don't like this, Saburo."

"We'll be OK," Saburo whispered.

"Not if Raahi is holding the cards. I don't trust him at all. Did you see his face when I mentioned that the box might be a genii jar? He's planning something, Saburo, and it isn't good. I wonder if we can wrestle the box away from him."

"But the oni gave him that box. This is his mission."

"The oni wasn't a bit happy about handing that box over to Raahi," Kate said. "He didn't trust the kid either."

"But he had to do it," Saburo said, "and there must be a reason."

"A good one, I hope," Kate muttered. She held on to Tanuki and watched as the swirling black mass dropped to the ground.

21

Raahi's Downfall

BLACK WISPS BROKE from the cloud and settled to the ground. The wisps congealed into tall, dark men dressed in swirling black robes.

Raahi gulped. He wondered which ifrit was the leader. His hand grasped the silver box and he tried to prod Bakeneko away from the others. The camel wouldn't move.

"Come on," he hissed. "For once, do what you're told."

Bakeneko glared down her nose at the boy and sent a calculated wad of camel spit right into his face. Saburo snorted, and Kate whispered, "Serves you right, Raahi."

Raahi fumed and wiped the spit away. He couldn't wait to leave these kids. But how could he escape from Bakeneko's back? He struggled to slide off, but he remained stuck like glue.

By the time the ifrit had congealed, Raahi could no longer glimpse the towering sandstone buildings carved into the cliffs. The tourists scscrambled for the nearest shelter, hunkering down in any crevice they could find.

The ifrit turned to face the djinn.

Raahi scowled as Bakeneko followed the other camels. They inched away until the djinn blocked the children from the oncoming ifrit.

Aali turned to them. "This is not your battle. Stay here and we will protect you."

"It is our battle," Kate said. "You said it yourself. You were waiting on us to get here. We're supposed to help you win."

"But not yet," Aali said. "Right now, we need to protect you. Your part will come later."

Kate glared at him. "After you lose to all those ifrit?"

"We will not lose."

"Then we don't even need to be here," Kate said.

Aali gave her a grin. "Oh yes, I believe you do. But not to defeat this army. Just to defeat Shaitan."

The two armies advanced. Raahi wasn't sure what to expect. Neither side had any weapons—no swords or maces or guns—and they didn't let out any war whoops or battle cries. They approached each other in an almost friendly way. One genii from each side strode between the two armies to meet in the middle.

"Aali isn't the leader," Kate said.

Raahi nodded. Even though he had called the army together, Aali stood with the other djinn. A gold-cladded genii strode out to meet the ifrit leader.

"That must be Shaitan," Kate whispered, pointing to the swirling mass of black.

Raahi scrutinized the ifrit. Taller than the rest, a black turban concealed his face. Raahi couldn't determine what he looked like. But then, Shaitan raised his head and turned toward the boy. Raahi's throat went dry. The ifrit's red eyes burned right into him. The gaze shifted to Raahi's pocket. He had an unsettling feeling Shaitan knew exactly what lay stuffed inside. Raahi covered the box with his hand, as if that might protect it.

His mind raced. What would stop this ifrit from just plucking the box from his pocket? How could he bargain with such a powerful being? How could he have even thought he could stand up to this magnificent genii?

"Raahi," Kate said, "now might be a good time to ask Aahi how to use the box."

But Raahi gulped. "No," he said, "I know what I have to do."

"You do?"

Raahi nodded. He was lying; he had no clue as to what he was supposed to do. Kate might guess this, but he didn't care. He wouldn't ask for help.

"You're fighting against closed-mindedness, just remember that," Kate said. "It's the last of the Three Poisonous Delusions and it's yours."

A hum began over his head. Two reporter helicopters hovered there. This fight with the ifrit would make the world news. The djinn glanced up as well, but must have decided the helicopters were unimportant. They focused their gaze on Shaitan and their leader, who stood facing each other.

"What are they doing?" Saburo asked. "They're just standing there."

Raahi squirmed. He didn't like the eerie silence filling this place. Even the tourists had stopped their screaming and huddled against the cliff with fear-filled eyes, glued to the proceedings. He hated this. Anything would beat sitting here while the two djinn waged their staring war. He'd even welcome a full-out battle to this unnerving silence.

But then, a strange humming filled the air—a different hum than the rotors on the helicopters. It sounded like a huge nest of angry bees and it came from the two armies. Their lips didn't move, but their eyes blazed in fury and the humming increased. Raahi gripped his ears. This sound was ten *times* worse than the shrieking of that demoness back in Bhutan.

Before he could blink, the genii armies charged each other and melded together. The ifrit turned into black wisps and the good genii morphed into dazzling sprays of silver and gold smoke. The colors blended together and turned into a swirling mass that rose into the air and headed towards the scrambling helicopters.

Bakeneko lowered herself into a kneeling position and Raahi slipped off her back. Now he must act. Kate and Saburo still sat glued to their camels. They couldn't help him. Now was his chance to do what he needed to do.

What *was* he supposed to do? He gazed at the humming, swirling ball above him, and then at the columns ahead. The beautiful building carved into the cliff was called the Treasure House; he remembered that from the TV show. A light filled the open doorway. It glowed a deep red, like a fire. Raahi gulped. Something compelled him to move that way. As much as he had dreamed about visiting this place, he didn't want to enter it now.

But he had no choice. His feet led him to the portico and up the stone steps. What he thought was fire wasn't, for the red glow warmed his skin but did not burn him. He stepped into the empty chamber and looked around.

The red glow cleared. Raahi gasped and stumbled, falling to his knees.

Mounds of treasure covered the floor. Gold coins, glinting jewels, silver goblets, and precious vases filled the room. More treasure than the biggest vault in the largest museum could possibly hold. And a voice echoed through the chamber, or was it in his head?

This can all be yours.

Raahi licked his lips. His hand snaked towards a stack of coins. He grabbed a handful and watched as the coins sifted between his fingers like sand trickling through a sieve.

This could all be his. But at what cost? His hand moved to the pocket where the silver box lay. He glanced towards the doorway, expecting to see the speaker. But he only saw swirling sand. His eyes turned to the treasure. He blinked.

The treasure had vanished. The room became as black as night.

Raahi's nerves took over. He hated dark, confined spaces. He crawled toward the exit, ready to head outside. But instead, he crashed into a solid rock wall where the exit should have been.

He sunk to the ground. He had been drawn into a trap. And he had no idea how to escape it.

"Where'd Raahi go?" Saburo said.

Kate yanked her eyes away from the mesmerizing but completely confusing battle overhead. "He isn't on his camel?"

"No. I don't see him anywhere."

"Well, that's just great. He's supposed to fight these guys. Do you think he ran away?" Her eyes turned towards the Treasure House. "Bakeneko's gone too. Last I saw, they were both headed to that building. Do you think they went in there?"

Saburo shrugged. "Maybe. If Bakeneko let him off her back, then maybe he was supposed to go that way. Maybe Shaitan is in there, and that's where Raahi has to fight him."

Kate frowned. "I don't like this, Saburo. I mean, I think Raahi is a pest, but he needs our help. I always need help; even you needed my help when you fought the demoness at the Chortens. How do you think Raahi's gonna fare all by himself? He needs us."

"Well, my kitsune isn't letting me off," Saburo said. He shifted his weight, but couldn't throw his leg over the camel's back. "She doesn't want me helping, I don't think."

Before Kate could say anything else, the humming increased and drowned her out. She gazed up, wondering which way the battle would go. Would the good djinn win? Or would the evil ifrit defeat them and take over?

And if the ifrit won, what would happen next? Without Aali's side backing them up, she and Saburo were sitting ducks. They only had their spirit guides to protect them.

Tanuki started moving. He lolloped towards the huddled, frightened tourists. Kate glanced behind her. Kitsune followed Tanuki. Why were they heading this way? Then she understood.

"Get out of here!" she yelled to the fat cowboy. "Those black things up there, they're evil genii. They feed off human's souls, and if they win, they'll be coming for yours. Get out, and take these tourists with you."

The cowboy managed to convey the message to the tourists near him, and they headed away from the battle. Kate's camel shuffled around the city as she yelled at the people crouched in crevices.

"Get back to the gorge! Run! You can get out of here if you go that way. If you stay, those ifrit will get you."

By the time the genii tumbled to Earth, all the tourists had made a dash for the gorge and the exit to the desert. Kate sat on a stone step, exhausted. She had done her best for the people, but what about her and Saburo? What would happen to them?

And where on Earth had Raahi gotten to?

22

Reunion

RAAHI DIDN'T KNOW what was happening. He blinked, but couldn't see anything except blackness. A cold fear gripped his heart. His worst nightmare had come true. He was lost in the dark, with no hope of escape.

His breath came in shallow gasps and although he tried to stay calm, the panic built up so fast he could hardly control it. He didn't dare move. What if he stepped into a hole or a chasm and couldn't get out? He cowered on the floor, legs curled up and hands covering his head. He waited for the end. While he waited, he choked out loud sobs and let his tears stream onto the cold floor.

After he couldn't cry anymore, he looked up. His heart leapt as he spotted the exit. He scrambled towards it, halted, and backed up.

This wasn't Petra.

As scared as he had been in the chamber, Raahi hesitated to leave it now. He stared out the doorway to a place foreign, yet strangely familiar. He definitely had left Petra. He was someplace different. But where?

Suddenly, Raahi wished for the others. They annoyed him, they angered him, but they had still stood by him. They'd even helped him, although he hated to admit it. Tears welled in his eyes. What he wouldn't give right now for Saburo's gentle smile. Or even Kate's haughty laugh. Anything would be better than this terrifying quiet.

A soft mew echoed through the darkness. Raahi's heart leapt as he turned around. Bakeneko sat behind him. She purred, swished her tail, and fixed her mesmerizing green eyes on his brown ones. He had never been so glad to see anything in his life.

"You came," he whispered. "Thank you, Bakeneko."

He caressed her fur for the first time and marvelled at how soft it felt. She purred louder and rubbed her huge head against his palm. Raahi flung his arms around the giant cat and cried until Bakeneko's fur was soaking wet and he had no more tears to shed.

Then he stepped out the doorway. A hot sun swept over the dry, dusty landscape. In the distance, a beautiful domed structure rose behind a muddy, churning river, its tall minarets poking into the blue sky. The Taj Mahal. He was back in India.

He sucked in his breath, excitement coursing through him. He turned to Bakeneko, grinning.

His heart froze.

Shaitan stood there, his cold, red eyes glaring at the small boy. A twisted smile played on the genii's face as he took a menacing step forward.

<<<◇>>>

"KATE," SABURO SAID. "I think we're winning."

Silver and gold streaks with just a few wisps of black made up the rolling genii ball. Saburo was right. The good genii had defeated the ifrit.

"Aali called it," Kate said. "He said they'd win."

"He also said we'd need to defeat Shaitan after this part was over," Saburo said. "But where is Raahi?"

"He went into that building, I just know it," Kate said. "C'mon, Tanuki, let's check it out."

But Tanuki refused to budge.

The mass of swirling colors congealed into several exhausted genii. Aali hobbled towards them.

"What happened to the ifrit?" Kate said.

Aali gave her a weary look and sat in the sand. "We've sent them away. It has drained my magic. I'm afraid I won't be much help against Shaitan. He escaped us. Now is the time for you to act."

"Yes, but how?" Kate said.

Aali frowned. "You were sent here and you do not know what you are supposed to do?"

Kate shook her head. "We just had a little silver box to fight Shaitan with, but it's gone now. Raahi has it and we can't find him. We think we went into that building over there, but we can't check. Our camels won't let us go."

Aali's eyes widened. "A silver box?"

"Yeah, do you know what it is? Raahi was supposed to ask you, but he never got around to it. Hey!"

Aali had whipped around and bolted towards the Treasure House. He ran inside, but came back quickly.

"He isn't in there, but I sensed deep and evil magic in that chamber. I fear Shaitan has taken the boy."

Saburo, who hadn't liked Raahi at all, frowned. "Oh no."

"Do you know what the box was for?" Kate said. "Was it the way to defeat Shaitan?"

Aali studied her. "If I held the box, I might know. If I had studied it just for a little, I might have guessed at its purpose. But I'm sorry. I have no idea what your friend's box does."

"We thought maybe it was Shaitan's prison. Like in the stories. Geniis can be trapped in jars and have to grant wishes to whoever lets them out."

Aali shook his head, a small smile on his lips. "No, I'm afraid it doesn't work that way. But two things are certain here. Shaitan has escaped and he's taken your friend with him."

"Probably what Raahi wanted," Saburo mumbled.

"But not what he'll be happy for," Aali said. "If he thinks he can make a bargain with Shaitan, he's wrong. Shaitan is ruthless. He will never bargain; he will take what he wants. Your friend is doomed."

"We've gotta save him," Kate said. "Where do you think he went?"

The genii rubbed his chin. "The ifrit have a few strongholds scattered through the world. Places like

Petra where they've gathered in the past. Your friend, what country was he from?"

"India," Kate said.

Aali frowned. "I cannot go that far. But maybe you can. There is enough magic left in the chamber to send you to where Shaitan and your friend went. But I don't know if I have the strength to send you there. And I do not know how you could possibly defeat Shaitan."

"But you said before that we were meant to defeat him," Saburo said. "That's why we came here."

"Yes," Aali said, "but I planned to help you."

Tanuki picked that minute to shape-shift from the camel to his normal, hairy self, and Kate fell into the sand, coughing. "Well, they've changed back. I wonder what this means."

Saburo pointed to the Treasure House. "Kate, look!"

Kate lifted her eyes, screamed, and bolted toward the high columns. Saburo followed her.

A thin boy and a tall girl stumbled out of the Treasure House. They stared around with wide eyes.

"Pietro! Jinjing! Where've you been? We've been trying to reach you forever." Kate threw her arms around the girl, and Saburo shook the boy's hand.

"Well, for the last two days anyway," Saburo said. "What are you doing here?"

Pietro grinned. "We're here to help you, I guess. Where are we?"

"We're in Petra. You just missed the big genii battle. But Raahi's gone now, and we have to find him."

"From what you've told us, he isn't worth finding," Jinjing said.

Kate frowned. She still didn't like Raahi much, but he was part of their team, and they had to find him. Plus, he had the box. "Yeah, but the world's safety depends on it."

Jinjing rolled her eyes and laughed. "It always does. So, what do we have to do?"

"You must go back into the building from which you came," Aali said to Jinjing. "I will try to send you after the boy. But I need help. My magic isn't enough."

Behind him, Tanuki butted the genii with his head. Aali looked down and smiled. "Maybe your help will be enough," he said to the spirit. "Let's go."

"I don't get it," Saburo said, as they moved towards the Treasure House. "Where did you two come from?"

Pietro laughed. "Let's just say we've had a crazy couple of days, and it'll take a lot of explaining. We'll tell you about it later. But for now, what do we have to do?"

"I will send you after the boy," Aali said. "Your spirit guides will use their magic to strengthen mine, and together we can get you there."

"Will they come with us?" Kate asked.

"Yes. They are not finished guarding you yet. But how you will rescue the boy, I do not know."

"Can we use this?" Jinjing asked, holding out her hand. A small jar lay on her palm.

Kate grinned. "You brought Pandora's box."

Jinjing laughed. "Somehow, I had this feeling it would come in handy."

Aali took the jar and opened it. "This is an ancient jar. It contains many magical properties." He ran his finger along the jar's empty insides. "I think I may know how this can be used. But not to beat the ifrit."

"Then what can we use it for?" Kate asked.

Aali frowned, then his lips curled into a smile. "Kate, you showed me a magical object once."

"Yes," Kate said. "My lipstick tube."

"And do the rest of you have objects like this?"

Saburo pulled out his spoon. Jinjing raised her barrette in one fist and Pietro held up his water bottle.

"Put them in the jar," Aali said.

All the objects fit except Pietro's bottle. Aali took it, held it in hands, and mumbled something. Pietro's bottle shrunk to the size of a thimble.

"You can grow it back, right?" Pietro said. "I could never use that to drink out of."

"Of course," Aali said, putting the bottle with the other objects. He closed the lid, gripped the box in his large hands, and chanted in a sing-song voice. The box glowed.

"What do you think he's doing to it?" Kate whispered.

"He's enchanting it, obviously," Jinjing said, "but for what purpose, I don't know."

Aali opened the box. "You have used these magical objects before, yes?"

"Yes," Kate said.

"You can use them in the same way now," the genii said.

"Oh, cool," Kate said. "You mean the whole fire and water and food and weapons dealy-o?"

Aali nodded. "With these, you can fight the ifrit, release your friend, and capture the jewel. But you must hurry. Your friend does not have much time. Stay close, now."

He handed the magical objects back and motioned for the animal guides to join them. They huddled in the middle of the room as Aali chanted over them. The room went dark.

"Jinjing," Kate whispered, "It's good to see you. And you too, Pietro."

Jinjing grasped Kate's hand. "A lot has happened since we talked last. Do you think we can save the boy?"

Kate smiled. As much as Raahi annoyed her, she didn't want anything bad to happen to him. "He had to fight closed-mindedness and he lost," she said. "I wonder *how* he lost. But I know this, Jinjing. I had to fight my own demons once too, and I lost. And you helped me win. If there's a way to help Raahi, we have to find it."

She gripped Jinjing's hand and with her other hand she reached for Saburo. The four friends closed their eyes and waited. Whatever lay ahead, together they'd make it. They would save Raahi, defeat Shaitan, and get the jewel back. They were together and they were strong.

23

The Showdown

RAAHI BACKED AWAY, but he couldn't go far. Behind him, a stone wall protected him from a hundred foot drop to the river below. In front stood Shaitan, his lips curled over his teeth in an evil grin. Raahi's heart pounded and he realized that all his thoughts had been foolish. He could not bargain with this demon. More importantly, he found that he did not *want* to bargain.

What he wanted were his friends.

Maybe they weren't friends yet. Maybe it would take some time for a true friendship to grow. But for the first time in his young life, Raahi had been a part of a group. He had always pretended that he had friends before. All his lackeys who did his every bidding weren't really his friends. He always treated them as inferiors and, now that he thought about it, they probably hadn't liked him at all except as a leader. As a good evil bully, he had never trusted any of them.

But he realized that for all his complaining about them, he trusted Kate and Saburo. He wondered if they were happy that he had disappeared. He knew they didn't like him much. And he understood why. But he had a feeling they would try to rescue him anyway.

Shaitan stepped towards him. "Give me the box, boy."

Raahi gulped. Now that it came down to it, a fierce desire to protect the box gave him strength. "No," he said. "You can' have it."

Shaitan's grin spread. A gold tooth glinted in the sunlight. Raahi kept his eyes locked with the ifrit's. His heart, which had been clenched in fear, began to flutter in excitement. He had seen a movement behind Shaitan's flowing robes. But he didn't want to give it away.

"You have heard about the ifrit, yes?" Shaitan's voice came out as oily and smooth as butter. "The ifrit need to feed on human souls to gain strength."

Raahi could think of nothing more horrible than losing his soul to this evil genii. But his fear kept decreasing. Both of Bakeneko's tails swished into his vision. He wasn't sure, but he thought he saw something else behind the big cat.

Shaitan was only steps away. His red eyes glinted. He stretched out his hand.

Raahi jumped sideways as Bakeneko leapt onto Shaitan's back, propelling the ifrit forward and flinging him right over the stone wall to the river far below. The boy couldn't help whooping with glee as four kids pelted out the doorway. Kate and Saburo were there along with a skinny boy, but Raahi's eyes locked on the massive girl towering over them all. She wielded a huge, glinting sword, and she looked ferocious.

"Where'd he go?" she yelled.

"Over the edge," Raahi said, "but I don't think that'll stop Shaitan. He can fly."

Kate pulled up to a stop beside the boy and peered over the wall's edge. "You OK, Raahi?"

"I am now. Thanks, Kate."

Her eyes fluttered to him, surprised. "You're welcome."

"Who's the girl with the sword?"

Kate grinned. "That's Jinjing. But I don't think we've got time for introductions. Here he comes."

Raahi backed away. This wasn't his fight. Kate, Saburo, and the new boy (Raahi figured he must be Pietro) strung out in a line behind Jinjing.

"Jinjing!" Kate yelled. "What do we do?"

"My sword can't fight that smoky thing," Jinjing said, watching the black wisp that was Shaitan as it swirled towards them. "Pietro! Your water bottle!"

"*Si*," Pietro said. He opened his bottle and aimed it at the black wisp. Raahi wasn't sure what came out of the bottle, but it wasn't water. It shot out and propelled Shaitan backwards. The droplets fell hissing to the ground.

"Acid," Kate said. "Stay back, Raahi."

A high wail echoed across the river as the acid scattered the smoke into the air. "He didn't like that," Jinjing said.

"Look." Kate pointed to the wall, about twenty feet away, where the genii now morphed back into solid form.

"The acid'll keep him from turning back into smoke," Jinjing said. "Kate, you're up."

"Right." Kate pointed her lipstick tube towards Shaitan and held on with both hands as a white-hot blaze shot from the tube and exploded against the ifrit's armour.

"Keep it up!" Jinjing said. "Saburo, go!"

"What should I do?" Saburo asked, staring at his spoon. "It just makes food."

"Do what you did last time. Make that stirring motion. Kate, keep it up. He's trying to turn back into the smoke. Pietro, fire that acid at him again. If we can keep him in some kind of arrested form, this'll work. We've just got to hold him."

Saburo swirled his spoon in the air. The ifrit's screams echoed off the walls. Raahi wasn't sure if he was screaming in pain or anger. But he couldn't move. As long as the kids kept up their attack, Shaitan was stuck.

Raahi wondered how long they could hold him there. And what would happen next.

Saburo's spoon kept Shaitan's body twirling in a tight spin. Pietro's acid prevented him from returning to his wispy form, and Kate's fire sucked out his strength. Raahi watched, fascinated. Little by little, Kate's flame shortened, and the swirling genii drew closer.

"Raahi!" Jinjing yelled. "The box!"

Raahi jumped, startled. He pulled the box out of his pocket and opened it. The box flew forward, dragging him towards the ifrit. What was happening now? The box was acting like some strong magnet, with Shaitan as its attractant. He stumbled forward, holding on with all his might.

"Pietro, let go," Jinjing said. Pietro closed his water bottle. Raahi was glad. The box had dragged him past the Italian boy, and he sure didn't want to get hit with any of that burning acid. His arms felt hot, though. Kate's fire was much too close.

"Kate," Jinjing said. Kate closed her tube. The fire stopped. Saburo still swiveled his spoon, and the genii still spun.

"Raahi, now!" Jinjing yelled.

And Raahi didn't hesitate. He didn't worry about what might be in it for him, he didn't bristle at getting ordered about by somebody else. He jumped forward, and the box sucked the swirling mass into its innards. He slammed the top shut. The box grew so hot he almost dropped it, then it slowly cooled.

"So it *was* a genii prison," Saburo said, panting and gazing at the box. "Aali was wrong."

"Well, maybe he didn't know," Kate said. "He didn't seem to know much. Although, he did know enough to re-magicate our objects."

Jinjing laughed. "Re-magicate?"

Kate grinned. "Hey, the word fits. What do we do with Shaitan now?"

Raahi put the box in his pocket. "We'll take him to Amaterasu."

"What about the jewel?" Saburo said. "We don't have it yet."

"I bet you do," Jinjing said. "I bet it's in that box, along with your ifrit."

Kate smiled at Raahi. "Good going, boy. You had us scared there for a while. We thought we'd lost you."

Raahi couldn't help it. He smiled. "Bet you would have liked that."

Kate punched him in the arm. "Well, you are a pain. But so am I. So, if you can put up with me, I can put up with you."

Raahi exhaled. He hadn't realized he'd been holding his breath, wondering what her answer would be. He felt that he should offer a sincerer apology, but wasn't sure how to do it. Kate didn't seem to mind. She understood.

He turned to Saburo. "Thanks, Saburo."

Saburo nodded. "*Daijobu.*"

"What?"

"He says it's OK," Kate said. "So what do we do now? I mean, are we splitting ways again? We've gotta go back to Japan and deliver Raahi's ifrit, but I'm not sure how you'll get there, Pietro. Or Jinjing. You don't have spirit guides."

"Not ones that'll take us back to Japan," Pietro said, "but we can get back home easy enough."

"How?" Saburo asked. "How did you even find us?"

Pietro glanced at Jinjing, and she smiled, her eyes twinkling.

"Well, it's kind of a long story, Pietro said. "I think it'll have to wait until we meet again."

24

War of the Gods

RAAHI APPROACHED THE goddess. Any thoughts of keeping the jewel had vanished. He placed the box on the rock and backed away, bowing.

"You have done well," Amaterasu said. "All of you."

"Ma'am," Kate said, "Um...miss...oh man, I'm sorry, I have no idea how to address a goddess, but can you answer my question now?"

"What question is that, child?" Amaterasu said with a smile although Raahi had a feeling she already knew.

"Why are we here? Why are we doing this? Why is all this happening?"

The goddess floated to the rock and picked up the box. "In this box you have captured one of the evil ones, the ifrit Shaitan. He is only one of many, I'm afraid."

"Tell me about it," Kate said. "There were tons of those ifrit thingys running around."

"No," Amaterasu said, "there are many evil gods like Shaitan. He is a minor god, but he is powerful. And now he is captured. His ifrit will not be so much of a problem, as long as Shaitan does not escape."

"What about the jewel?" Saburo asked. "Is it in there too?"

"It is. We will have a tricky time getting it out, without releasing Shaitan. But as long as we hold the box, the ifrit can't get out. His people are leaderless. That is one less army we have to worry about."

Raahi gulped. "There's more?"

The goddess nodded. "I'm afraid this is just the beginning, but you have struck a major blow. So have your friends."

"Jinjing and Pietro?"

Amaterasu smiled. "They have been very busy the last couple of days."

"Must've been why we couldn't get in touch with 'em," Kate said. The goddess nodded and turned to leave.

"Wait!" Raahi said. "You still haven't told us why we're doing all this."

Amaterasu turned. She looked pensive, as if unsure whether she should, or would, tell them — mere mortals — about the business of gods.

"We do have a right to know," Kate chimed in. "After all we've been through."

Amaterasu's brother, Tsukiyomi the Moon God, stepped out of the wood. "You do," he said. "But we cannot tell you the whole story. Even we do not know.

We know we were trapped on our island and couldn't leave. We know that if we had not been able to get our treasures back, the enemy would have become that more powerful. We know we have many enemies out there. But someone, we don't know who, is bringing the evil gods together. He is massing forces. And he must be stopped."

"Wait," Kate said. "Did you say: 'we *were* trapped'? Are you not trapped anymore?"

Amaterasu's smile was almost joyous. "We are not. Your friends fixed that problem."

"They did?" Saburo said.

"We are going to have to have a serious talk with Jinjing and Pietro," Kate said. "They've got some explaining to do, that's for sure."

"But you still don't know who is causing all this?" Saburo said.

"No. All we do know is that our world is in danger and so is yours. And you three…you *five*…are our only hope for stopping it."

"Whew," Kate said. "Way to put a burden on somebody."

"The two worlds are merging together," Saburo said. "Why?"

Tsukiyomi rubbed his chin. "We do not know. But we do know it will cause chaos, for both your world and ours. There is a reason why the two dimensions are kept separate. They can't coexist. If the worlds are merged completely, it will mean the destruction of us all."

Raahi sunk to the ground. This was too much. The full realization of this task stunned him. He looked at Kate and Saburo. Kate frowned and Saburo sighed, but neither seemed as afraid as he. Maybe because they were more used to these types of adventures. He decided that if Kate and Saburo could ask a question, he could too. He asked the question that had been bugging him since they left Bhutan.

"The screams," he said. "The demoness at Dochula Pass, I could hardly stand her screams. But the others could. Why? Why couldn't I stand the screams?"

Amaterasu smiled. "You fought closed-mindedness."

"Yes. But I didn't do very well."

"Not at first. But you opened your mind and heart in the end. You opened them to friendship. To trust in other people. If you met the demoness now, her screams would not affect you as badly. You would have your friends to buffer the sound. As it was then, nothing shielded your heart, and that is why she terrified you so."

Raahi nodded. He wasn't sure he totally understood. But he felt better.

"Trust in each other," Amaterasu said, "and you will succeed. You will conquer the demons. And you will bring this war to an end."

Her brother nodded. "But now," he said, "you must go home. The capture of Shaitan is a blow to our enemy, and it will give him pause. Rest while you can although your rest might not be as peaceful as you might hope."

"Yeah," Kate said. "We're gonna have a lot of explaining to do when we get back."

Raahi glanced over to Bakeneko, who rubbed against Tsukiyoma's legs. "Can our spirit guides come with us?"

"Not if it's anything like last time," Kate sighed, scratching Tanuki's head. "We'll have to leave them here."

Saburo nodded. "And Kitsune has her ninth tail. Her wisdom is now complete."

Raahi glanced at the others. "I wish I could talk to you when we get back," he said. "In secret, like you can do with your magical objects."

Saburo frowned, and Raahi wondered if the boy was still mad with him. But then Saburo said, "Raahi, I don't think you'll need a magical object."

"Why not?"

Saburo's face broke into a grin. "Well, I've been talking in Japanese since we got here, and you've understood everything I've said."

Raahi gulped. "Really?"

"Hey yeah!" Kate said. "I put my lipstick tube in my pocket after the fight, and Saburo hasn't touched his spoon. And I could understand you too, Saburo." She turned to the goddess. "Does the magic only work here, in this glade?"

"No," the goddess said. "No, you will always be able to understand one another now, no matter what language you speak. It is our gift to you. Our thanks."

<<<>>>

COMING HOME WAS different this time around. After her last adventure, Kate's father had been none the wiser, and she had resumed where she had left off, as normally as possible. But now, three things had happened.

Kate's father had been absolutely frantic with worry, and she couldn't blame him. They'd been gone five days at least. He had missed both the fight in Bhutan and the meeting with the Rollin Calf, but the fight with the ifrit had made national news, and at that point he realized his daughter was mixed up in something he couldn't possibly wrap his mind around.

He still couldn't. He kept staring at Kate, like she might blink out of existence at any minute, and even though she had told him everything she knew, he didn't quite believe her. She even showed him the videos of the demoness and their excursion to Jamaica, but he just shook his head, gulped down some aspirin, and had to lie down.

The other problem was the press. The press lurked at her doorstep, and after a few run-ins with less-than-pleasant reporters, Kate wanted nothing more than to crawl under her covers and not come out at all. She almost wished the gods would call her back into their weird world, just so she could avoid the paparazzi.

But, that became her third problem. The more she thought about it, the more nervous Kate got. It didn't help that almost every day now some new sighting made the news: a mysterious object flying through the air in China that looked eerily like a dragon, a strange glow emanating out of every crumbled building on top of Machu Picchu, the Loch Ness Monster breeching out of its watery den and smashing a fishing boat with its tail. All sorts of oddities were popping up, and the reporters gravitated back to Kate every time something happened. It was like they thought she had the answers. But she didn't.

She had no idea what was going to happen next.

SABURO HAD IT even worse. The Japanese press dubbed him the "Miracle Boy" and they continually aired his story. He became an instant celebrity even though all he wanted was to huddle on his mountaintop alone. He could run up the mountain now without a hitch in his stride, and his family still hadn't gotten over the shock. Neither had Saburo.

"It still feels strange," he said to Kate. They talked on a regular phone now because they could understand each other perfectly. Sometimes Saburo spoke in English, just to practice, but he wasn't sure if Kate could tell the difference. Either way, she understood him.

"Isn't it fun to run, though?" Kate said. "And jump and stuff?"

"Yeah, it's great. I just can't get over it though. Kate, this is driving me nuts."

"What, the leg?"

"No, the waiting. I'd rather get this over with."

"Yeah, me too. How's Raahi holding up?"

"Pietro talks to him more than I do," Saburo said.

"I think it's pretty cool that Amaterasu's gift somehow got to Pietro and Jinjing too," Kate said. "It's nice that we can all talk to each other and not have to use our magical objects. But it's funny that Raahi would want to talk to Pietro. They don't even know each other."

"Pietro says they have a lot in common," Saburo said.

Kate sighed. "Well, I agree with you about wanting to get this all over with. A part of me wishes the gods would hurry up and call us again, but a part of me hopes it never happens."

"Yeah," Saburo said. "I know what you mean."

RAAHI STROLLED DOWN the dusty street. Two small boys walked towards him. When they saw him, they both froze. He smiled.

"Hello."

The boys shrieked and ran down the street. Raahi sighed. He was trying to be nice, but it didn't seem to work. With his new-found fame, kids were even more fearful of him. Even his bully friends cowered when he approached. He felt like an Untouchable, all alone with no one to talk to.

But that wasn't quite right. He had his four new friends.

"It's terrible," he said to Pietro. "How do you put up with all this attention? Do people treat you like you're somebody with a horrible, contagious disease?"

"Well," Pietro said, "it's not so bad for me. Half the people in my town don't believe any of what I've told them. Nobody caught my and Jinjing's adventure on video, and I used to lie all the time, you see. So, all my friends still think I'm making it up even though I'm not. It's hard to ditch a reputation once you've created it."

Raahi sighed. He liked talking to Pietro. Even though he hadn't gotten to know the boy very well, he felt he had more in common with this kid. True, Pietro was no bully, but he still struggled with getting over his past. So did Raahi.

Trying to be good wasn't always as easy as it sounded.

"Tell me about your adventure with Jinjing," he said. "Amaterasu said all the good gods were imprisoned in their own lands, but now they're not, thanks to you. How'd you do it?"

"Well, it was a scary mission," Pietro said, "but parts of it were pretty amazing, just like your adventure. Anyway, it went like this..."

About the Author

ORIGINALLY FROM VIRGINIA, Nikki Bennett avidly read C.S. Lewis, J.R.R. Tolkien, and any book that had to do with fantasy while growing up. After spending the first part of her "adult life" on a farm raising horses, she and her husband Steve (who drew the artwork for this book) moved to Japan. There, Nikki developed a love of Asian mythology and history. In 2015, they moved back to the U.S. and now reside in Washington state.

Three Treasures is the sequel to *Four Fiends*, and is the second book in The Countdown Chronicles. Keep reading for a sneak peek of *Two Portals*, the next book in the series!

Check out Nikki's other titles at:
www.bennettcreativeservices.com

If you enjoyed this book, please tell your friends and post a review at Amazon.com! And if you'd like to follow more of Nikki's adventures, check out:
www.patreon.com/bennettart

Thanks, and keep reading for a Sneak Peek of the next book in the series: *Two Portals*.

Pietro's Walk Home

Pietro stared at the bull, and the bull stared back.

It was black as coal. Two sharp horns poked out of its skull, and angry red eyes glared at the boy across Signore Falcone's rickety fence. If that bull wanted, it could rip the fence down with one toss of its pointy horns.

Cutting across Signore Falcone's pasture was the easy way to get to Pietro's house, and the fun way too because he had to dodge the bull. On a normal day, the bull ignored the boy. Once, on a dare, Pietro had even climbed on its back. The bull had flung Pietro off and went back to chewing grass like it had swatted an annoying fly away.

Today, the bull pawed and glared at the boy. Pietro tried to think back, but he only remembered that bull having dull brown orbs, not flaming red eyes. He placed a hesitant foot on the lower fence board, wondering if he should dash through the field like usual or take the long way home.

The bull swished its tail and snorted. Steam poured out of its nose.

Steam.

Pietro lowered his foot to the ground. He fumbled for his water bottle and yanked it off his belt. He took a big swig of water to wet his dry throat, then put the bottle to his lips and whispered, "Hello? Can anyone hear me?"

If another kid had walked by, that kid might have laughed at Pietro trying to talk into a water bottle. But Pietro had a secret. Last year, magical dragon had enchanted his bottle, and he could talk to three of his friends through it. Those three friends had joined him on an incredible adventure then, and they had magical objects too.

Jinjing lived in Hong Kong and she kept an enchanted barrette pinned in her hair.

Kate lived in America. She carried a magical lipstick tube.

And Saburo, who lived in Japan, had a tiny wooden spoon on a keychain. When Saburo held the spoon in his hand, he could talk to the other kids too. And it didn't matter that he spoke Japanese, Pietro talked in Italian, Jinjing in Mandarin, and Kate in English. When they talked through their magical objects, they could all understand one another perfectly.

"Hello?" Pietro said again. He hoped someone would answer. Right now, he knew that Kate and Saburo were off on a crazy adventure rescuing three sacred Japanese treasures from some terrible fiends. He and Jinjing had been left behind. He had wondered why.

Now he thought he knew.

A girl's voice echoed out of the water bottle. "Pietro? Is that you?"

"Jinjing! Where are you?"

"I'm heading to Macau for the weekend with my grandfather. What's going on?"

Pietro locked eyes with the bull. "I think something is happening here."

"In Italy? Really? What?"

Pietro licked his dry lips. "You remember me telling you about that bull I rode when I was little?"

Jinjing snorted. "You mean the one that threw you off as soon as you sat on it?"

Pietro couldn't help grinning. "That's the one."

"And?"

"I think it's possessed."

"You do?"

The bull stared at him with an intensity he'd never seen in its normally dull eyes. It perked its ears, as if it were trying to hear everything the boy said. Pietro lowered his voice to a whisper.

"It's got red eyes. And it snorted steam a second ago. And it won't stop staring me. Usually it ignores me like I'm a pesky insect."

"Is it possessed in a bad way, do you think? Or a good way?"

That question wouldn't have made much sense to most kids, but Pietro understood what Jinjing meant. He had met both good and bad spirits on his last adventure. The trick was to decide which spirit you could trust and which was about to try and chop you into mincemeat.

"It doesn't *look* friendly."

"Then stay away from it. I've gotta go, Pietro, my grandfather is calling for me. I'll talk to you in a bit."

Pietro clipped the water bottle onto his belt and decided against cutting through the bull pasture. He jogged along the road instead. The normally lazy bull snorted and picked up a trot, keeping pace with the boy as he ran along the fenceline.

"Go away," Pietro hissed.

But the bull didn't. It kept trotting, its red eyes locked on the boy. Pietro made a decision right then and there that the bull was bad news.

If he could have run away from the pasture, he would have. But the pasture fence ran along the left side of the road and a sheer cliff tumbled off the right edge, all the way to the Adriatic Sea frothing against the rocks below. Pietro could only move forward or back along the fence line, and forward was closer to home. The bull would have to stop when Pietro passed the end of the fence.

Or would it?

The huge animal snorted and veered closer. Pietro leaned forward, scooped up a rock without breaking stride, and flung it at the bull's shoulder. It hit with a THWACK! The bull didn't flinch. It moved so close, Pietro could almost reach out and touch its sharp horns.

He let out a yell and pelted forward as fast as he could. He wasn't good at much, but Pietro excelled at running. Even a massive bull would have a hard time keeping up with his fleet feet. He reached the end of the fence and kept going. Past the bull pasture lay his father's olive orchard—and home.

The bull's stomping hooves stopped. Pietro slowed and glanced behind him. Then, he skidded to a halt.

The bull was gone. It had paced him to the end of the fenceline, but now it had disappeared.

Pietro prided himself on his bravery. He had often boasted to others about it, but now he didn't feel brave at all. That bull could be anywhere. Hiding behind an olive tree, crouching behind a rock; it didn't matter how big it was, if a spirit was possessing that bull, Pietro didn't doubt it could shrink or grow to any size it wanted. Spirits could do that sort of thing.

He ran through the orchard and barrelled into the house, almost smashing into his brother Luigi.

"Watch where you're going," Luigi yelled.

Pietro didn't respond. He careened into his room, slammed the door, and grabbed his water bottle.

"Jinjing, are you there?"

"I'm here. We just got off the boat. Gong-gong went to get a cab. What happened?"

"It's definitely a possessed bull. It was there one second, gone the next."

"Where do you think it went?"

"I don't know. Jinjing, do you think…"

Tap-tap-tap. Tap-tap-tap.

Pietro stiffened and turned around. The bull's horns scraped against his bedroom window. Smoke billowed from its nostrils and fogged the glass, which shattered as the bull thrust its head into Pietro's room and bellowed.

Pietro stumbled to the door. He flung it open and dashed into the main room, smashing straight into Luigi this time.

"Pietro, you stupido! Watch what you're…"

The bull's roar drowned out Luigi's rant.

"What was that?" Luigi screamed.

"Run!" Pietro said, scrambling to his feet. "It's Signore Falcone's bull."

"What? What did you do to upset the bull, Pietro?"

Pietro didn't have time to lecture his brother about the problems with evil spirits. He shoved Luigi towards the safety of the kitchen and then glanced over his shoulder. The bull had already charged through his bedroom door. It must have shrunk to fit through the window and doorway, but now its massive frame filled half the main room and it was only inches away. It put its head down and pawed the floorboards.

He couldn't outrun such a powerful and possessed beast. Pietro stared into its red eyes, almost mesmerized by them, until something even brighter flashed in the corner of his eye. He turned his head a millifraction.

From the fireplace, a golden light streamed through the air and smacked the bull on its forehead. It roared and backed up a step. Pietro turned his head fully now towards the fireplace, his heart pounding.

A green flame shot out this time, landing on the bull's forehead. Its horns lit up like a Christmas tree.

The bull howled, backing up so fast it left hoofmarks in the floor.

A bright red flame leaped from the hearth and exploded onto the bull's chest. One more howl and the bull vanished with a POP! that shattered a wine bottle on the table and caused three plates to fall off a shelf and crash to the floor.

Pietro took a couple of deep breaths. He tried to slow his pounding heart. He turned to face the fireplace and whatever new demon lurked there.

But he didn't see a demon. Instead, a tiny, fat man sat on the hearth. The man wore a bowler hat and had his teeth clamped on a pipe. Bright sparks popped out of the pipe. The little man waved at Pietro.

"Well," the man squeaked, "he didn't like *that* now, did he?"